DETERMINED

The TRUE STORY of BIG BLUE WALKINGHOOD

Luman C Slade

With Illustrations by Anita Harmon

ISBN-10: 1482562421

EAN-13: 9781482562422

I dedicate this book to my wife, Jeanette,
and to my Grandson, Avery.
Both provided invaluable assistance
and encouragement.

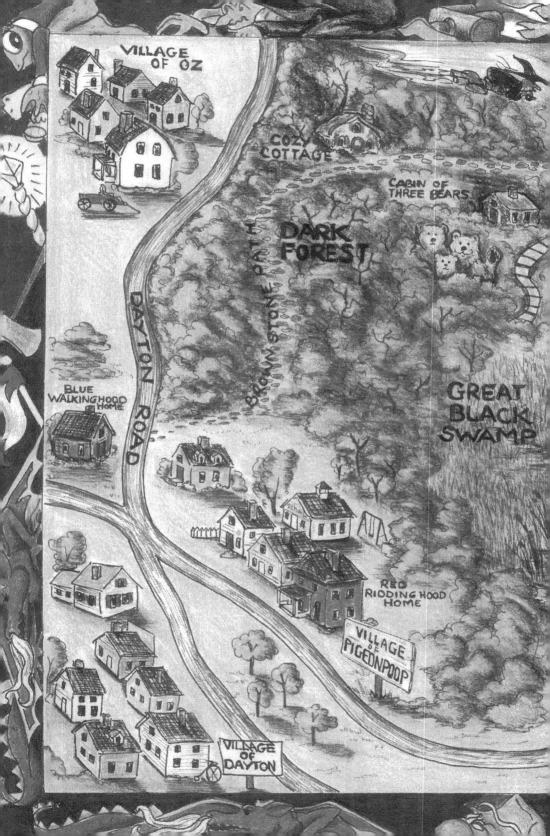

GREAT SHAKEY MOUNTAINS
HOME OF WICKED WITCH OF EAST
SPITEFUL TRAIN TRACK
BILLY GOAT BRIDGE
GNOME TRAIL
STORY LAND
CASTLE OF UNCLE WIERDO
PIGEONPOOP ROAD

CONTENTS

Determined: The True Story of Big Blue Walkinghood

Join Big Blue Walkinghood and her rival cousin Little Red Ridinghood on their heroic journey through magical Storyland. Experience their fears and joys as they encounter fairytale adventures by the dozen--each retold in a highly devilish format. Witness their startling encounters with wicked witches, big bad wolves, grimy gnomes, humongous spiders and other colorful Storyland characters. Feel the evolving emotions of the two young girls as they are brought together for a common mission.

The reader is taken back to the year 1895--a time when things were quite different--a time of invention and change, a time when language was dissimilar, a time when fairytales were called occurrences.

Determined combines history and fiction into a dramatic, heart-touching tale that is exciting, informative, and hilariously funny.

CHAPTER ONE

Cozy Cottage

Summer 1895

CHOP! CHOP! CHOP! Big Blue Walkinghood[1] had chores to do and splitting firewood was but one of them. At only thirteen she wielded an axe like she was Paul Bunyan's sister. With clenched teeth she raised her axe high and brought it down on a hapless log. CHOP! The earth shuddered.

There was something about chopping wood that excited Big Blue—that made her feel strong and proud. She was good with an axe and she knew it. She knew it could be used as a weapon, too.

In the year 1895 Dark Forest was a rugged wilderness, a mysterious and dangerous place--a place to be avoided. It was known to be inhabited by funky and sinister characters of every description: witches, wolves, gnomes, dragons, and monsters—just to name a few. It was infamous for its many incidents of bizarre happenings of the most dreadful kind: kidnappings, disappearances, curses,

---

1 Big Blue Walkinghood—definitely not to be confused with Little Red Ridinghood.

incantations[2], and transformations. And it was a remote place. So remote, in fact, it had never been penetrated by roads. Indeed, only a stone path meandered through its dark dense woods, hilly terrains and fast streams. That path in one direction led to the thriving village of Pigen-poop, and in the other to the legendary place called Sto-ryland.

Yet despite everything a young girl lived in that foreboding place. She lived there with her grandparents, Granny George and Grandpa Scaredypants, in a tiny dwelling known as Cozy Cottage. CHOP! CHOP! Big Blue Walkinghood was determined to split a half chord of wood before Grandpa's feeding time. She had no doubts she could do it however; once she set her mind to do something it was as good as done.

Her grandfather, before being cursed into a frog, had taught her about splitting wood, and about axe safety. "Keep your mind on the job every second," he cautioned her. "One *little* mistake could cost you a *big* toe, and in your case it would be...*a really big toe*."

Since moving in with her grandparents chopping wood had become a welcomed escape for Big Blue. It kept her from constantly worrying about her parents who were far away in Africa. They went there to search for a cure for her Grandpa's curse. The problem was their journey took them into dangerous jungles.

---

2 Incantations—the ritual chanting of magic words spoken as a spell.

Big Blue knew all about jungles. She read about them in Granny's encyclopedias. She learned that boa constrictors can swallow people whole; and people are killed by mosquito bites--it's called malaria. Jungles, the books said, are full of ferocious animals, deadly frogs, fire ants, poisonous snakes, flooded rivers, and killer bees. Her parents had been there for nearly a year and she knew their luck couldn't hold out forever. They just didn't understand how dangerous their mission was. She had to find a way to get them out.

But what could she do? And who was there to help? She certainly didn't want to involve her ancient grandparents who were more than seventy years old. With all this on her mind she was worrying herself sick. Sometimes she imagined hearing her parents calling out to her "Help, Big Blue, HELP!"

To ease her mind she went back to chopping wood. CHOP! CHOP! her axe rang out. With muscles straining she was an imposing sight. A stranger seeing her for the first time might say, "Wow!" Tall, straight, and stout, she was obviously not someone to be messed with.

Like her mother and her grandmother she was strong and robust. And just because she hadn't won any beauty contests didn't mean she was ugly. Indeed, some found her ruddy looks quite striking. Her grandfather liked to make her blush by telling her she was the most stunning lass in all of Dark Forest. Her handsome freckled face was somewhat hidden, however, by her tangled auburn hair, which she wore loosely. And, as you might expect, everything about Big Blue Walkinghood *was big*, especially her feet. Much to her dislike she had inherited the family trait of having large feet.

Now resting her axe she looked up at the sun. When it was straight up she knew it was noon, and that meant it would be Grandpa's feeding time. But as she looked up this time a movement caught her eye. Although the trees partially obstructed her vision it appeared to be a large, dark, ugly bird. It was pointed on top, wide at the bottom, and with a short thick tail. Yet how could it be a bird, she wondered? Don't birds always have wings?

Whirrrrrrrrrrrrrrrrr. "Rupppp rrupppp," it went, as it disappeared among the trees.

What kind of creature would make such an ugly sound, she wondered? Now she was really puzzled. She remembered hearing the sound once before, but hadn't seen anything that time. It must be something like a humongous buzzard, she guessed. Or maybe it was just her mind playing tricks on her. Whatever it was she decided not to mention it to her grandmother. Granny George had problems enough already.

After looking up at the sun again she realized it was, indeed, past Grandpa's normal feeding time. Knowing he would soon be getting jumpy she hurriedly emptied the contents of her bug collectors. She was happy to see there were lots of grasshoppers, which were Grandpa's favorite food. Feeding Grandpa Scaredypants was just another of her chores--but, like chopping wood, it was one of the chores she enjoyed. In fact, she liked anything that brought her close to her grandfather.

⟿ ⟾

Meanwhile, inside Cozy Cottage Granny George was fast asleep in her rocker, while Grandpa Scaredypants, as usual, was crouched under the dining room table. "CROOOOAAAAKKKK," went Grandpa, scaring the dickens out of Grandma.

"Huhhhh, whaaaasshhh sszattt?" she mumbled as she jolted awake. She fumbled about the side table for her spectacles so she could find her teeth. After locating both, she irritably asked, "WAS THAT YOU, GRAND-PA, YOU OLD POOP?"

"Croooooaaakkkkk, whooooooo elllse?" he replied in his shaky voice.

"Santa Claus!" she sarcastically answered. After a small chortle she stroked her chin whiskers and resumed rocking her chair...creak crack, creak crack. Soon her eyes sagged shut and she began singing her favorite song. The old hymn helped to take her mind off her troubles, she always said, "Amaaaaazing graaaaaaace, how sweeeeeet..."

In his crouched position beneath the table Grandpa Scaredypants appeared smaller than he really was. A curse by Wicked Witch of the East left him looking, and acting, frog like: with large protruding eyes, webbed fingers and toes, powerful legs, a glimmering green complexion, and an extra-large nose. His human brain, in fact, was his only feature that *wasn't* amphibian[3].

Although it had been nearly a year since his curse he was still far from being normal. The spell changed not only his features, but his behavior too. It made him terrified of almost everything—everything that is, except flies. At that very moment, in fact, he had his eye on a pesky fly.

"Zzzzzzzzzzzzzzzzzzzzzzzz", it went, circling closer and closer.

Grandpa remained stone still, except for his huge eyes--which slid back and forth in their sockets closely following the fly's path. Suddenly his long tongue shot out-- nailing the critter. "CROOOOOOOAKKK," his voice thundered from under the table.

"Did you snag another one?" Granny George asked.

"Youuuuuu betchaaaaaaaa," he proclaimed with a mischievous grin.

All was normal at Cozy Cottage...or was it?

---

3 Amphibian—a cold-blooded vertebrate animal. You would know had you stayed awake in Science Class.

CHAPTER TWO

Things Were Different Back Then

In the year of our story, 1895, things were quite different. The residents of Cozy Cottage, for example, had not witnessed the invention of radio, television, computers, airplanes, and yes even Lego. There were no school busses, either. Instead, children walked to their schools—often uphill both ways. Just one teacher taught all of the grades.

But those were also exciting times. New inventions and discoveries were constantly in the news. Automobiles were beginning to appear in nearly every village. Bicycles were so popular they created traffic jams. Just a few years earlier, 1n 1876, Alexander Graham Bell invented the telephone. At the time of our story, however, telegrams were still widely used.

Language was different too. People enjoyed showing off their large vocabularies. Granny George, for instance, liked using odd and colorful words such as rambunctious, balderdash, gobbledygook, thunderation, gibberish, goodness gracious, fiddlesticks, and mercy sakes. Some people suspected she had swallowed a dictionary.

There were more witches, ghosts, monsters, vampires, sorcerers, and other scary creatures back then, too.

Dwarfs, gnomes, goblins, and munchkins were so plentiful it was hard to get around without tripping over them. Human encounters with those characters were recorded in books that are now called fairy tales.

Unfortunately, over many generations of re-telling many of those stories have become so twisted they are now barely recognizable. In fact, much research is required to get to the truth of those tales[4].

Yes, things *were* different, but then again maybe not *that* different. Just as today people in that era had good times and bad times. Big Blue Walkinghood was no exception. Up until the time her parents left she was a happy child. And even though she was the class giant and somewhat awkward she did have friends--just not *best* friends.

There was Linda, who liked to play softball. And there was Jackie, who liked to go fishing even more than she did. And there were two brothers: Orville and Wilbur, who were always tinkering with bicycles--making them into all sorts of contraptions. She liked both of them, but secretly liked Orville best.

Everything changed, however, the day her parents left. Even after they had been gone for months she still couldn't believe they had abandoned her. Now she was isolated from her friends, separated from her parents, and she no longer went to school with her classmates.

---

4   A good research source is, "Disregard Those Cracked-Up Versions of Fairy Tales," by Humpty Dumpty.

THINGS WERE DIFFERENT BACK THEN

Her life now evolved around nothing but Cozy Cottage. It wasn't that she didn't love her grandparents--she did. But they were not the same as her parents, her friends, or her classmates.

Her worrying began almost immediately after they left. She couldn't stop thinking something awful was going to happen. Even her dreams were terrifying. In one, she dreamt she had gone to Africa to find them. After days of following their tracks she finally caught sight of them. They were in a makeshift raft on a swirling river filled with crocodiles. The raft jolted in the raging currents while her mother and father struggled to hold on. Then it tipped over, sending them bobbling around in the fast waters. The horrible nightmare jolted her awake--screaming, crying, and shaking.

The nightmares continued. It got so bad she hated going to bed. The lack of sleep, and her worrying was changing her behavior--making her mean and irritable. She wasn't proud of herself when she was like that, but she was having trouble dealing with it.

That pompous Wizard from Oz had assured her father the trip to Africa would only take a couple of months. Yet nearly a year later they were still gone. Something was drastically wrong and she felt it was her responsibility to rescue them.

And, as if that weren't enough, there was another problem--the telegrams had stopped. Her parents hadn't sent one in over three weeks. That had never happened before. To Big Blue it meant one thing: trouble, big trouble.

⋯⟞◉⟝⋯

THUMP THUMP THUMP, went Granny George's cane as she tromped into the kitchen. Her thumpity cane prevented her from sneaking up on anybody. After waving her hand in front of Big Blue's face, she said, "Are you going to just stand there with a blank stare on your face, or are you going to feed Grandpa?"

"Oh!" she answered. "I'll take care of it, Granny. I like being with him when he eats. When he's done he always lets out a silly croak just to make me laugh." With that, Big Blue joined her beloved Grandpa under the table, presenting him with his favorite dinner: grasshoppers fried in garlic butter.

She liked spending time with him down there in his secure place, and she knew he liked having her there too. Even though his frog vocabulary was limited, she patiently listened and understood him better than anybody. She realized, too, that he *was* gradually improving. Every once in a while he would add another word to his vocabulary, even though it would often be mixed in with coarse croaking sounds.

Although she didn't agree with her parents about their search for a magic cure for her grandpa's scaredyness she still hoped there was one. In one of her dreams her parents had found the cure and they were on a steamship headed home. Maybe, she liked to imagine, they wanted to surprise her, and that's why they hadn't sent a telegram. But the more she thought about it the more she had doubts.

Unlike her parents she wasn't convinced the cure Magnificent Wizard told them about would work. Instead, she believed Wicked Witch of the East was still controlling him--restricting his transformation. The witch, she believed, had to be destroyed in order to release him from her control. But how to do it was the question.

"CROAAAAAAAK!" went Grandpa, scaring the heck out of Big Blue, who had drifted off into deep thought. "Hee hee hee," he went, with a tired-looking grin. It was time for his nap so she kissed him on his nose and tucked his teddy bear up close.

Then she crept out to the porch where she pulled on her boots. Even though it took a lot of lacing, she loved her boots. They made her feel tough, and besides Grandpa gave them to her. "They may not be glamorous," he told her, "but they are practical. They'll help protect your feet when you're using an axe."

Granny George sometimes kidded her about her boots, calling them clodhoppers. Big Blue hated it when she said that, especially because her grandmother's feet were even larger than hers.

Yes, Granny George did have extra-large feet, but unlike Big Blue she was not ashamed of them. She believed a person should be happy with whatever God gave them.

"Big feet have their uses," she always said. "What if you need to stomp out a forest fire? Or what if there's a big snowfall and you don't have snowshoes? Or what if there's an invasion of ants?"

Now in her seventies, Granny George was a well-preserved specimen. She was stout as a stump, sharp as a thistle, and a good talker too. Her friendly hazel eyes gleamed when she smiled, which sadly, wasn't that often anymore. Her noggin[5] was covered with a goodly amount of ginger-and-white-streaked hair--which she wore in a single braid, and which complimented the faded freckles that adorned her face and arms.

Her most noticeable features were her husky build, inch-long chin whiskers, and, as already mentioned, her freakishly large feet. She used a cane crafted by Grandpa to get around, but only because a hiking accident had left her with a bum knee.

Like Big Blue, Granny George's life had become complicated by recent events. First, there was Grandpa's curse, which nearly destroyed him. Then, her daughter and son-in-law went off to a God-forsaken scum hole of a place on a poorly planned mission in search of a magic cure. And, on top of everything else, they left Big Blue, a mere child, behind to live with them--a couple of old fuddy-duddies[6].

---

5 Noggin—an old-fashioned name for head.
6 Fuddy-duddies—meaning old and unwieldy.

THINGS WERE DIFFERENT BACK THEN

But Granny George didn't like to dwell on *her* problems--she was more concerned about her granddaughter. Mindful of Big Blue's anxieties she tried her best to keep things on a positive note and to bring *some* joy to her life. Every morning, after home-schooling Big Blue, she made a habit of playing checkers with her. Then, in the evening she encouraged Big Blue to read to Grandpa. She could see it was the highlight of Grandpa's day, and Big Blue's, too.

Granny George, like Big Blue and Uncle Weirdo, hadn't thought much of the trip to Africa. She tried to tell her daughter that time and love were what Grandpa needed most, not some magic cure prescribed by some bizarre wizard. But they didn't see it her way and went ahead with their plans. She didn't complain too much, however, just on the chance they might be right. All she really wanted was for Grandpa to be the way he used to be, no matter what it took.

Before his encounter with the witch Grandpa Scaredypants was a strong and straight octogenarian with sea-blue eyes, wavy white hair, strong hands, and a laugh like rippling water. His warm smile and happy manner charmed everybody. Nobody could remember Grandpa Scaredypants ever having a bad word to say about anybody. He accepted people as they are and was generally a happy man--that is of course, before his encounter with the witch.

DETERMINED

16

Children especially loved Grandpa. They liked the tall stories he told and the way he could wiggle his big ears to make his hat bounce up and down. They liked it too that he thought like they did—daring to believe in his dreams. Yes, Grandpa chased his dreams by living like a pioneer--forever exploring Dark Forest and its mysterious surroundings. He knew all about the woods, Grandpa did. He hunted wild game, fished the streams and rivers, collected wild mushrooms, and built shelters so he could survive in the woods for days at a time.

And who was his outdoors pal...his constant buddy, always at his side? None other than his beloved granddaughter, Big Blue Walkinghood, that's who.

⊷≡◉≡⊷

And at that very moment his granddaughter had just rested her axe. Her thoughts immediately wandered to her parents. Why, she wanted to know, did they listen to that arrogant wizard? If they hadn't listened to him they would never have gone to that awful place called Africa.

CHAPTER THREE

Magnificent Wizard

ig Blue Walkinghood was with her father the day she first laid eyes on Magnificent Wizard. He was the one who told them about the tree that could cure Grandpa of his scaredyness.

It was on Wizard Day that her father, for the first time, took her with him to Oz for the gala celebrations. The village was bustling with vendor carts, horse-drawn carriages, bicycles, and even a steam-powered tractor. Bands played marching songs, merchants hawked their wares, and women showed off the contents of their perambulators[7]. Big Blue was simply giddy with excitement.

The event was named after Magnificent Wizard himself. He had organized it to bring the commoners together. "By trading together," he told them, "we will bond lasting friendships and will all prosper."

For his role in the festivities he had constructed a circus wagon pulled by eight perfectly matched white goats. What a grand scene it was to see its arrival. Carnival music blared from a calliope[8] played by a

---

7 Perambulators—baby carriages.
8 Calliope—steam powered musical instrument (similar to an organ).

properly-dressed monkey. TOOT! TOOT! went a whis-tle, followed by a cannon shot, BOOOOOM! Bushels of popcorn magically fell from the sky.

Up on the very top of the wagon in a king-sized chair sat the orchidaceous[9] Magnificent Wizard him-self. Impeccably dressed, he wore a purple suit, pol-ished black boots, a red shirt, and a yellow and black polka-dot bowtie. A red, white, and blue top hat rested on his impressive head, only partially covering his long silvery hair. His plumb shaped nose and huge protrud-ing belly were the only distractions to his otherwise dignified appearance.

Wizard's two burly aids, dressed as clowns, tossed out candies to children along his route. Wizard waved a scepter[10] carved of ivory and tipped with a large dia-mond, above his head, as if bestowing his blessings. The pricey jewel reflected dazzling light beams over the ex-cited crowd.

His whole purpose in life, he proclaimed, was to help people. And to do that his huge wagon was equipped with bins, cupboards, and barrels to house his large inven-tory. Banners informed shoppers of his merchandise and services. They read: Psychoanalysis, Constipation Cures, Curses Undone, Warts Treated, Remedies for Every

---

9 Orchidaceous—meaning extremely showy or a flaunting show of wealth.

10 Scepter—a ceremonial wand used as a symbol of authority.

Malady[11], Toes Straightened, Tattoos applied, Tattoos Removed, Flatulence[12] Cures, Ears Pierced, Keys Made, Magic Potions, Hard Candies, Rheumatism Relief, and much more.

When the fabulous wagon came to a halt The Great Wizard stood tall and chanted to the onlookers, "Have no fear, Wizard is here! Wizard is here! Wizard is here!" The assembly cheered in appreciation, whistling and hooting as they hurried to his wagon. His aids handled the more mundane transactions, reserving the pricier ones for the great ones' personal management. Silver, gold, and paper money gushed to the wagon like a fast flowing stream.

Jack Walkinghood, Big Blue's father, took note of the banner that read, Curses Undone[13]. "I wonder," he pondered, "if Wizard could help Grandpa. Maybe there's a cure for his scaredyness. It wouldn't hurt to inquire."

"But Father," said Big Blue, "He seems like a big buffoon[14]..."

"What did you say?" asked her Father. "It sounded rather impertinent."

"I'm sorry Father," said Big Blue, "It's just that..."

"Not another word, Young Lady," he scolded.

---

11 Malady—old fashioned word meaning sickness.

12 Flatulence—meaning gas, windy, tooty.

13 Curses undone—in 1895, even as today, many people put their trust in wizardry and black magic.

14 Buffoon—somebody behaving in a silly way.

"Wizard, Sir," said her father, "I'll get right to the point. My wife's father has been cursed by a witch. He escaped from her, but is still suffering from the spell. I beg you to help us if you can."

"If I can?" How provokingly awkward you pose that question. Of course I can; I'm Magnificent Wizard! Have you been living with your head...uh... in a barrel?"

"Beggin' your pardon, Sir," said Father. I only meant to say..."

"Fret not," said Wizard. "I understand the situation, but you haven't disclosed the type of curse your father-in-law is afflicted with. Out with it, Man, is he a lizard, a newt, or what?"

"A frog, Sir, she turned him into a frog."

"A frog, huh? He's still a frog?"

"Well, he's somewhat better, but still a long way from being normal. He hops around croaking all the time... and he's afraid of everything."

"Gurgling gargoyles! That's a bad curse all right...but there is a remedy. It hinges, however, on finding...hum-mmm... a certain rare tree. The tree's common name is...... I think...antifearall. Let's see," he said as he fumbled through a box of papers. "Here it is."

To Big Blue it looked like he was only holding a clipping from a newspaper. She almost spoke out, but after glancing at her father, decided to bite her tongue.

Her father held out his hand.

"Hold on, Jack!" Wizard sharply said, "Did you think I would simply hand it over? Obviously you have no idea how valuable such secrets are. In fact, I must constantly be on guard against witches, ghosts, and other scoundrels who would love to get their slimy mitts on them. My aids may play the role of fool clowns, but trust me, Sir; they are formidable adversaries for such fiends. You see, I can't help the lowly masses unless I'm first made safe from the evil elements of this world."

"But I digress," he continued. "Getting back to business, the leaves from that tree can be ground into a powder, that when mixed with other secret ingredients is more powerful even than the mighty frog spell. I might reveal to you the secret of the tree's location but it would cost you dearly."

Even though everybody seemed to trust Magnificent Wizard, Big Blue had trouble understanding why. For some reason she just didn't like him, and most of what he said sounded like a lot of hooey. If he's so great, she thought, why would he demand payment for doing a good deed? A good deed should be its own reward, Granny always taught.

"Just...just...how much money are we talking about here?" her father hesitantly asked.

Wizard glanced around, wiped his brow, and then whispered, "Understand, Good Man, I could be tarred and feathered for releasing such secrets. Besides, I'm not convinced you could keep the matter confidential— or afford the price."

"You know we're desperate," Father retorted, "How much, Sir, how much?"

"Six thousand dollars," slid off his tongue like an ice cube off a stove poker.

"Good Lord!" said Father. "That's a fortune. I couldn't even come close. Have a heart, Sir."

"It's because I have a heart that I can make the offer at all, Good Man. Understand this; wizards live by a code. And if we break the code we're done, finished, and kaput[15]. Trust me, my prices are always fair. But perhaps you haven't considered other ways of financing. How about your home, do you own it?"

"Y...y...yes," Father nervously answered. "But...but... at most it's worth...maybe, five thousand."

"Because you are a good and honorable man, Jack, I would be willing to take title to your little property as payment in full."

"...Uh...uh...fair enough," said Father. "It's a deal-- as long as my wife agrees. I don't know how we'll get by without a house, but finding a cure for Grandpa is worth more than any house in the world."

"You're a rare gem, Jack," said Wizard. "In order to close the deal you must come back no later than four o'clock tomorrow--with title in hand."

"But...but... I'll need some time; I've got to talk to my wife."

---

15 Kaput—done, finished. Yes, I do know about redundancy.

"Tut-tut[16]," said Wizard. "I don't have time for trivial talk, others are in line. You know the terms, now be gone with you."

Her father's proposal was received by her mother no better than if he had vented a toot[17] in church. "Are you out of your mind?" she screamed. You've got mush for brains." On and on they wrangled until the wee hours of the night. Big Blue put cotton in her ears and went to bed.

Something miraculous must have happened that night, however, because everything was better in the morning. They enjoyed a peaceful breakfast together, possibly because nobody talked.

⊷⧸⊜⧹⊶

At noon on the following day Jill and Jack Walkinghood, title in hand, met with Magnificent Wizard.

"The first order of business," he said, "is signing over the title. After that I will give you this bag of condiments to be mixed with the antifearall leaves, and specific information as to the rare tree's whereabouts."

After completing the legal matters he said, "You may want to take notes because I dare not give out these secrets in written format. Look for the antifearall tree

---

16 Tut tut—meaning impatience, not twin Egyptian Kings of ancient times.
17 Toot—Meaning a windy sound, followed by smelly vapors; often occurring around young boys.

around Mount Killray, in the province of Canga, which is on the continent[18] of Africa.

"Having located that tree," he continued, "grind two pecks of its' leaves into a powder and combine it with the contents of this packet. Finally, place this concoction, along with a kettle of fresh cat scat, and a cuspidor[19] of bulldog spittle into a cauldron. Boil for thirty-three minute only. Your patient should be given daily doses of seven liters for nine days. Side effects could include headaches, bloating, belching, runny nose, slobbering, tooting, vomiting, sudden death, pimples, and uncontrollable diarrhea. Take only as directed. The warranty is valid for ninety days.

"That's not much of a warranty, Sir," Jack Walkinghood complained.

"An astute observation," Wizard said. "I can offer an extended warranty for only ninety-nine dollars and ninety-nine cents...cash."

---

18 Continent—a main landmass on the globe. Special note: the words continent, incontinent, and consonant are easily confused. An old Welsh legend tells the story of Sir Dumkin the Slow, a knight in the Court of King Ivan ll. The king put him in charge of a brigade and sent him north, commanding him to not return until he found more continents. Some forty years later Sir Dumkin and his men returned with wet and stained britches that reeked of pee and poop, and a book titled, "Ffjjrd, Llnnd Fff Lll Nrrrt", which contained not a single vowel. When questioned about new land masses, Sir Dumkin shamefully confessed he had found none. It seems he had confused continent with incontinent and consonants.
19 Cuspidor—a large bowl for spit; widely used prior to drinking fountains.

"Never mind!" said Mother. "We can't afford it."

And with that the affair was completed. Wizard scurried away with the deed tucked into the lining of his hat, while Father remained in his chair clutching a small smelly knapsack.

Just five days later Big Blue's parents boarded a ship headed for Africa. They traveled light so they could move fast. While they were gone Big Blue would be living with her grandparents at Cozy Cottage. For safety reasons it had been decided that she would be home-schooled by Granny George.

Big Blue desperately wanted to go with them, but they wouldn't consider it. "Jungles are no place for children," her mother said. "And besides, we're counting on you to take care of Grandma and Grandpa while we're gone."

She felt like she had been run over by an ox cart. She was crushed...and she had the terrible feeling she would never see her parents again. She understood though, why they went: Grandpa desperately needed help.

Taking care of Grandpa was a big job. Just finding enough insects to feed him every day was a major chore. Big Blue was happy to do it though; she would do anything for Grandpa.

One thing she discovered about being with Grandpa was that, like chopping wood, it helped her to take her mind off her parents. It was a relief to have a few minutes each day not worrying about them.

Of course Big Blue loved Granny George just as much as she did Grandpa Scaredypants, but her love for Grandpa was special. From the time she was four years old she spent her summers at Cozy Cottage... where she was Grandpa's pal. He taught her about the outdoors, Grandpa did: about making fires, building shelters, survival, tracking animals, fishing, hunting, and much, much more.

She loved to think about those good times with Grandpa, but it made her furious when she thought about what the witch had done to him. She had the feeling the witch was still controlling him. One of her ideas for getting her parents back, in fact, was to find a way to destroy her. With the witch dead, she reasoned, the curse on Grandpa would go away--and her parents would have no reason to not come home.

CHOP! CHOP! CHOP! went her axe, as she made more firewood. She was proud of her skill with an axe... and she knew it could be used as a weapon, too. When she sank the blade into a log she sometimes thought about the witch. She swore if she ever got a shot at her she would show her what she could do with an axe...CHOP CHOP CHOP.

CHAPTER FOUR

Telegrams Spell Trouble

Nearly a year had passed since Big Blue's parents left for Africa. For Big Blue each day seemed like a lifetime. In their last telegram they reported they were going to a different part of the jungle, across the Wilde River. They said a medicine man told them about a new place to look for the elusive "antifearall tree". They would be leaving the next day, her mother wrote, in order to get there before the monsoon rains begin. "Don't worry about us, Darling," she said, "we will be very careful."

Big Blue grimaced and her heart pounded wildly as she read the message. It felt like her terrible nightmares were coming true. And, like the two telegrams before it, this one was totally confusing. The first one reported they were going south, and then they were going west, and now north. Why, she wanted to know, should it be so hard to find a stupid tree? Wizard assured them it would be easy.

Even with her grandmother's assurances that everything was going to be all right, she knew better. Her Grandmother didn't know as much about Africa as she did. And now she wanted to know even more. After waiting for her grandmother to fall asleep she quietly removed encyclopedias "A" and "M" and headed for the woodshed.

The woodshed was her private place. It was where she went to work out her problems. But as she sat on a log with book "A" she started shaking...and sobbing. She felt like her world was falling apart.

Her sobbing only stopped when she heard a new sound, "tk tk tk." She looked up to see a chipmunk on the wood pile. It was only a few feet away, yet it boldly stared at her, and chattered: "Tk tk tk."

"Hellow, Little Chippy", she said, holding out her hand.

"Tk tk tk," it answered, as it disappeared among the logs.

Wiping away tears she opened the "A" book to "Africa". In the pages about jungles she found what she was looking for: "The Wilde River Jungle," she read, "is one of the densest and most inhospitable places known to man. Very little is known about the southern part since its dense forests and extensive swamplands make it almost impenetrable. At the northern fringe, however, Mount Kilray rises to over eight thousand feet. Rich copper deposits were worked there in the early 1800's. In the 1850's gold was discovered south of the mountain near the present day town of Tea Bag. Early miners there reported a surprise finding of native Indians who still practiced head-hunting..."

Big Blue slammed the book shut. The information was even worse than she had expected. She hesitantly opened the "M" book to monsoon. "Monsoon," she read, "is a period of heavy rainfall due to opposing wind patterns caused by temperature differences..."

She stopped reading. Why, she wondered, would anybody go to such a horrible place? And why didn't she try harder to stop them?

And to make matters worse she was becoming bored to the max at Cozy Cottage...and was getting crankier by the day. It just wasn't fun living there anymore. After only a few months, in fact, it began to gross her out. Nothing ever happened that didn't happen every other day: chop firewood, collect insects, do home-schooling, feed Grandpa, fill his water bowl, help with the cooking. Wow! What fun!

Big Blue had another problem--a secret one--one that she never talked to anybody about. Her problem was that she never in her whole life had a really close friend. Not just an everyday friend, but a best friend: someone who stays by you no matter what, someone you can trust your life to, someone you can share secrets with. That's the kind of friend she longed for. But after years of disappointment she came to realize that big clods like her could never have best friends. The best she could ever hope for was to have any friends at all.

And now she was missing her friends. She wanted to invite them to Cozy Cottage for an overnight but she knew they wouldn't be allowed to go anywhere near Storyland. It had been so long since she had seen them she was afraid they would forget her. And every day she was away from them made her lonelier, sadder, grouchier, and meaner.

Then, on one otherwise uneventful day the tranquility was interrupted when Orville from the telegraph office rang the bell on his bicycle, RING! RING! RING! "SPECIAL DELIVERY!" he shouted.

Orville, at age fourteen, was one of the tallest boys in the ninth grade, and one of the smartest too. With sandy brown hair, brown eyes, and a trim physique he was popular with the girls, even though he was somewhat nerdy.

"Who is it for, Smarty Pants?" she asked. Actually she was happy to see him but she didn't want him to know it.

Orville looked hurt. He wondered why she was being rude. They had been friends for a long time. It made him angry that she was so fickle. His father had warned him, however, about the unpredictable nature of girls. "Son, get used to it," he counseled, "One minute they love you and the next minute they hate you. That's just the way girls are."

"It's for Granny George," Orville answered...retorting, "Not for you, Big Foot."

"Just give me the telegram and hold the lip, Orville," she snapped back as she grabbed it out of his hands. Lately she had noticed changes in him. He was getting wimpy, and she didn't have much use for wimps. Besides, he didn't like the same things she did.

Even though he was a grade ahead of her in school and got straight A's, he was still stupid as far as she was concerned. He didn't know anything about useful things: like fishing, hiking, or hunting...and he knew nothing about tracking animals. He didn't know bear dung[20] from deer pellets[21]. He didn't know rabbit poop from nincompoop[22].

She never told anybody that he had asked her to go to the seventh grade roller skating party with him. She refused, hoping somebody else would ask--but nobody did. The one thing she did like about him was that he was even taller than she was. He was good at basketball, too, and wasn't bad looking either--in a nerdy kind of way.

---

20 Bear dung vs. deer pellets. To discern the difference between bear dung and deer pellets, as every woodsman knows, take a deep smell of each. The one which causes you to pass out will be the bear dung.

21 Deer pellets—meaning deer poop. Marble sized brown-colored balls of dung resembling chocolate covered raisins. Caution: No matter what people might tell you, chocolate candies do not grow in the woods.

22 Nincompoop—a fool or simpleton. Someone who might eat chocolate candies found in the woods.

She glanced at the telegram. They're always so official looking, she thought. Without thanking Orville she signed for the delivery and turned toward the cottage.

"Can't we talk," he said. "I want to tell you about this bike I'm motorizing."

"Sorry, Orville," she said, "this might be important. I have to go."

"You're being very rude, Miss Bigfoot," Orville taunted as he rode away.

"Come on back, Orville," she yelled, "and I'll kick your butt with my big foot."

After blurting it out she wished she hadn't. It came out kind of dumb. Even though she knew Orville was right about her being rude she wasn't going to admit it. She rushed inside and handed the telegram to her grandmother.

"Whasssssssssh issssssssssss?" Granny George mumbled as she sat forward in her rocker.

"It's a telegram, Granny. Put your teeth in...then put your eyeglasses on...and...

"Awwwww rieeeeee, Mishhh Shmarrrtypannns," she said, "hoad yo haussssses." She plugged in her teeth, affixed her spectacles, stroked her chin whiskers, and then scrutinized the envelope as if it were a treasure map. Finally, frowning over the top of her eyeglasses, she said, "Humph, it's from Governor Billingsworth."

"Granny! Just read it, please! It could be about Mother and Father."

"Hold your horses, Honey; Grandpa needs to hear this too." BANG, BANG, BANG, went her cane on Grandpa's table. "GRANDPA! WAKE UP!"

Poking his nose out from under the tablecloth Grandpa Scaredypants's cheeks blew up like balloons, and he said, "CROOOOOOOAAAAKKKK, ohhhhhhhhhhhhh-hhhhhh kayyyyyyyyyyyyy."

"Very good! Grandpa, I understood you that time. All right now," she said, "here goes with the telegram[23]…"

Central Union Telegram

Granny George
The Cozy Cottage
Black Forest

Extreme difficulty. J&J Walkinghood/bad trouble. Missing 7 days. Heavy flooding/ferocious animals/ deadly snakes where headed. Last seen/Wilde River. Fearful place. Rescue & contact impossible. Warned not to go.
  Chin up/pray.
  End.

Governor Billingsworth, Canga, Africa

---

23 Telegram—by the year 1875 most of the continents were connected by telegraph cables.

With trembling hands Granny George dropped the telegram as if it were on fire. "Goodness gracious," she mumbled, "what an awful, awful message."

"Ohhhhhhhhh noooooooooooo," wailed Grandpa Scaredypants, tipping over his water bowl as he hopped back under the table.

"What does it mean, Granny, all that mumble-jumble?"

"Well, I suppose it's saying your parents are missing in the jungle and there's no way to contact them."

"That's what I thought it meant, but he's wrong. There is a way: Uncle Weirdo's invention. It works anywhere. Don't you remember his computeamajiggy[24]?"

"Honey," said Granny George, "facts are facts. The telegram said there is no way to contact them. My brother is an amazing person but I doubt his contraption can send messages to a jungle."

"BUT THAT'S WRONG, GRANNY, IT CAN!"

Granny George brought her rocker to a halt. With an upset look, she said, "Honey, please don't raise your voice to Granny. It's not like you to yell at me. Don't you think I feel badly too? Listen, things may not be as bad as you think. See, it only says, *they're missing*. That doesn't mean they're lost."

"I'm sorry, Granny. It's just that I'm so worried. Besides, how can they be missing unless they're lost? And jungles are bad places to be lost in."

---

24 Computeamajiggy—Uncle Weirdo's most famous invention. Forerunner of the modern computer.

"Honey, you're jumping to conclusions. One thing I've learned in life is that most things aren't as bad as they first seem to be."

"I'm going to Uncle Weirdo's castle no matter what, Granny. I have to! His computeamajiggy is the only way I can help them. It has maps, two-way mail, and lots of other features. He wrote me all about it."

"Honey, don't be ridiculous. How could a machine send mail without wires? How could it have maps of the whole world in it? And how would your parents receive the messages?"

"They have a receiver, Granny, Don't you remember? Uncle Weirdo made them take it with them."

"Yes, I do remember something like that, but I still have my doubts."

"But now you know, Granny, why I must go: so I can use his computeamajiggy."

"No! I'm not letting you go through Storyland alone and that's all there is to it. Not even if you were Flapperlady[25]."

"Noooooooooooooo," wailed Grandpa from under the table. "Don't goooooooooo, crooooakkkk." Any talk about Storyland, witches, wolves, fish, hawks, cats, and other scary things upset him tremendously.

"Settle down, Grandpa," Granny George pleaded. "Don't get excited, you know what it does to you."

---

25   Flapperlady—a heroine of early comic books; prior to Awesomegirl, Stretchlady, and Supergirl.

To Big Blue, she whispered, "Let's move out to the porch so Grandpa can't hear us." When they were outside, she whispered, "We're frightening him with all this talk, Honey. Your parents are smart people. I've got to believe they wouldn't go to that God-forsaken- place unless they had specific information. You know how important finding the cure is to them; they've been searching for nearly a year."

"I know...Granny," Big Blue whispered, "but I'm still going! You can't stop me!"

"Lord help me!" Granny George sighed, as she stroked her chin whiskers. Clomp clomp clomp, went her cane as she hurried back inside and sank down into her rocker, which meant she was considering things. "Leave me be," she pleaded, "I need time to think."

⊷══◉ ◉══⊷

Indeed, Granny George was faced with the hardest decision ever. Should she prevent her granddaughter from going on a dangerous journey, or should she stand by and do nothing to help her daughter and her son-in-law?

Creak crack, creak crack, went the old rocking chair. There would be a lot of creaking and cracking that evening.

CHAPTER FIVE
Granny's Dilemma

Creak crack, creak crack. Still in her heavy thinking mode Granny George had rocked her chair so hard it traveled half-way across the room before she knew it. Shaking from head to foot she clearly was a lady in distress. She knew something had to be done and she didn't like her options.

We should have moved away from Storyland a long time ago, she thought, before the silly place went bad. If we had everything would be different now. Grandpa would still be Grandpa, and not a fly-snagging half-Grandpa. Big Blue would still be with her parents and friends, not with a couple of old dinosaurs. And I would be knitting mittens instead of worrying my fool head off.

Forty-nine years earlier Granny George, or Georgia, as she was called then, and Bruce McGuire, her husband, moved into Cozy Cottage. The newlywed couple had stumbled upon it one day while hiking Brown Stone Path. Indeed, if Bruce hadn't left the path to follow deer tracks he would never have seen it; it was that engulfed by the woods.

What a sight it was: hidden by trees, vines, and undergrowth. Its stained cedar shakes, broken windows, and damaged chimney were a sad testimony to what it had once been. Yet its stout stone walls, green shutters, and beckoning carved door still hinted at its enduring charm.

The young couple checked the records and found the cottage had been built by a young man named Herman Waters. He was a naturalist and found the site to be an ideal place to pursue his studies in botany and zoology. Herman and his young wife Lola lived there for only a few years, however, before he mysteriously disappeared. The only evidence uncovered by the Sheriff was in the barn, where they found indications of a struggle and shreds of burlap. A manhunt ensued but failed to produce further evidence. A few months later Herman's parents' persuaded their daughter-in-law to leave Dark Forest and move in with them—leaving Cozy Cottage abandoned.

As is commonly the case in such doings, village fear-mongers spread the word as to what they thought happened. "It were a witch what took him," one old codger swore, "I seen it with me own peepers."

"Right!" his wife added, "It shore 'nuff were a witch… in a flyin' contraption."

That was all it took to convince the locals the cottage was bewitched. From that time on people steered clear of it like it was a skunk in the road. And after only a few years the cottage disappeared into the woods and was forgotten.

But as Georgia and Bruce explored the old residence a miraculous thing happened. The old shutters seemed to reach out to them, saying: "Welcome, please come inside. Here is where you belong. I need you as you need me."

Family and friends were dumbstruck when they learned the newlyweds had purchased the old place. "Why?" her mother asked, "would you want to live so far away from everybody? And why on earth would you choose to live next door to Storyland?"

As is often the case with young people the newlyweds didn't heed the advice of Georgia's wise mother. Instead they worked the labor of love to repair the place, which they named Cozy Cottage. They raised their daughters Jill and Harriet there and witnessed no serious problems. Sure, it *was* true Storyland was a strange place where all kinds of goofy encounters happened, but those encounters for the most part were exciting and even funny, and rarely were there harmful consequences.

One story was about the Pig Brothers. Two of their houses had been destroyed and the third had suffered serious damage. The Brothers claimed the damage was caused by a wolf, but the neighbors suspected it was really due to a storm. They believed the brothers were just squealing for attention.

Another story involved Miss Chickenlittle. She had filed an accident report claiming the sky had fallen--causing extensive egg damage. An investigation by the insurance company, however, found it was only tree branches.

Such happenings were common, and even expected, in Storyland. What wasn't expected was what came next.

First there was an incident with a young girl named Goldilocks. She had, without permission, gone for a walk on Brown Stone Path. She soon became lost and as darkness approached she took refuge in an old cabin. While there, according to her story, three bears nearly broke the door down trying to get her. The story got even weirder when she told about a flying dragon that came to her rescue. The dragon, she said, gave her a ride on his back and returned her home safely.

Then, only weeks later, a hunter reported shooting at a dragon of the same description. He thought he hit it but failed to bring it down. He estimated it was more than thirty feet long, and he swore it breathed fire.

The final straw, however, the one that caused people to alter their thinking about Storyland, was an incident that happened only two years earlier. Two highway workers that had been assigned to repair a bridge on Brown Stone Path mysteriously disappeared. The Sheriff found small human footprints left behind and signs of a struggle. But an extensive search failed to find a trace of the missing highway workers.

After that Storyland became a condemned place; a place of fear and danger. Even adults feared traveling there, and those who did went well armed.

And as time went by things got even worse. Confirmed sightings indicated that evil elements had moved in: ghosts, witches, wolves, bears, and gnomes[26].

⋯⇒◉⇐⋯

With all of this on her mind Granny George was trying to decide what to do. I have been so foolish, she told herself. Even after what happened to Grandpa, I was the one who refused to move. I have no one to blame but myself.

Indeed, family, friends, and neighbors had begged them to move out. Even before Grandpa's curse they had nagged them over and over. And now... their nagging voices had come back to haunt her.

"Move out of there immediately," her mother sternly advised.

"You'll be sorry!" a neighbor nagged.

Awakened from her disturbing thoughts, Granny George sat forward in her rocker and angrily blurted out, "I was stupid, I admit it. I'm just a stupid old fool."

"What?" said Big Blue. "Did you say something, Granny?"

"Never mind, Honey, I'll be with you in a minute." Granny George glanced over at her granddaughter. She's probably right, she thought. Uncle Weirdo's contraption may be our only hope. But what kind of grandma would I

---

26 Gnomes—legendary small hunchbacked humans who lived underground in burrows.

be to let a young girl go there alone. No! After what happened to Grandpa I just can't do it.

"Honey," she said, "I've come to a decision. I'm sorry but I can't let you go through that dreadful place alone. You know what happened to Grandpa...and that wicked old crone is still out there."

"Noooooooooooooooo," wailed Grandpa.

"You were eavesdropping, weren't you, Grandpa?"

"Nooooooooooooooooooo."

"You're a big fibber, too, Grandpa."

"Granny," Big Blue interrupted, "if you won't let me go alone, why don't you go with me?"

"Believe me, Honey, I would do just that if I could. But there's no way I'm going to leave Grandpa here alone. That old hag is still looking for him. She wants him back."

When Grandpa Scaredypants heard that he peed himself. "OHHHHHHHHH," he went as he jumped back in embarrassment.

"Then I'm going alone!" Big Blue said. "I'm not afraid of Storyland, or that witch. I'll take my axe with me."

"Don't get your knickers in a twist! You'll do no such thing! Be sensible, no one should go to that funky place alone. It's not just the witch either, there are other dangers."

"Granny, I love you and I respect your decision, but you leave me no choice. I have to go, and I will."

Big Blue's remark stunned her grandmother. She knew Big Blue well enough to know that when she set her mind to doing something nothing could stop her. But before she could say a word Grandpa interrupted.

"CROOOOOOAAAAAKKKKK" he belched, as if he was being murdered. His table jumped around as if it had springs on it. Big Blue rushed over—just as a chipmunk came scampering out with his tail sticking straight up. "Granny!" she yelled, "Look after Grandpa while I catch it."

CHAPTER SIX

Chippy

THUMP THUMP THUMP went Granny George, faster than most septuagenarians. When she reached Grandpa's hide-a-way she bent over and said, "It'll be all right, Grandpa, it's just a little squirrel. It can't hurt you."

"Yesssssssssssss itttttt cannnnnnnnnnnn," Grandpa retorted.

"Don't be silly, Grandpa, of course it can't."

"Cannnnnn tooooooooo," said Grandpa.

"You're a stubborn old goat, Grandpa, that's what you are."

"Crooooooooaaaaakkkk, ammm not," Grandpa said, having the last word.

Meanwhile, Big Blue chased the small squirrel around and around until she was dizzy.

Granny George laughed and laughed, "I know how to catch it, Honey, climb up a tree and act like a nut."

Big Blue finally trapped it in a corner and picked it up by the tail. It chattered and squeaked like a mouse in a trap. She held it in her hand and talked softly to it as she petted its head, "We meet again, little Chippy. No one's going to hurt you." She could feel its heart thumping as she held it, and she understood how terrified it was. She continued talking to it and petting it until its heart slowed down.

Then she took the chipmunk to the woodshed, "Maybe we can be best friends, Chippy," she whispered. She offered it some birdseed. "Are you hungry, little guy?" To her surprise the furry little rodent took a sunflower seed and stuffed it into his cheek pouch…then another…and another…and another…and another. His cheeks got bigger, and bigger, and bigger, until he looked like two balloons with a clown face squeezed in between. For the first time in a long time Big Blue had a big laugh. She laughed and laughed until tears streamed down her face. Then she cried…and cried.

"Are you all right, Honey," Granny George yelled.

"Yes… Gr…Granny… I'll be…right in."

She put Chippy down and placed a handful of birdseed near him. He went at it like a runt pig that was late for dinner. "I hope to see you tomorrow, Chippy," she whispered. "Maybe we can be best friends."

"Tk tk tk," went Chippy, shaking his head yes.

But she didn't go back inside. Instead she chopped more firewood. She wasn't ready to face her grandmother yet. After making more firewood she put her axe away and began thinking about her journey to the castle. I'll leave first thing in the morning, she thought. I'll take water and matches. And I'll hide my Swiss Army knife in my cape.

***

Inside Cozy Cottage Granny George was once again propelling her chair…and thinking. "She's going!" she mumbled.

"I know she is, and there's nothing I can do about it. Lord help me..........Amazinnnnnngggg graceeeeeee, how sew-wwwwt..."

She stopped when Big Blue entered. "H-o-n-e-y." she said, with eyes so red they looked like Christmas bulbs, "Come sit by Granny, I have something to say."

Big Blue shuffled over and sat on her footstool, waiting for what she didn't want to hear.

"H-o-n-e-y," Granny George said in a trembling voice, "I've reconsidered and I've decided on a compromise. Although I'm nervous about it I'm going to let you go... on one condition. Your cousin, Little Red Ridinghood[27], *must* go with you. She knows the way and she's wise about Storyland--especially when it comes to wolves."

"Oh no! Not Little Red. You've got to be kidding...she's..."

"Hush!" said Granny George. "Why on earth not? She's a sweet girl."

"But Granny, she hates me, and we're so different. She's so pretty with her golden locks, little red hood, and dainty feet, and I'm, you know...kind of big, and not so pretty...and I have big feet, and..."

"Nonsense! You are handsome enough. There's nothing wrong with big feet either. Big feet, big brain, I always say. Just look at mine! You are strong too—husky even. I love you just the way you are."

---

27 Little Red Ridinghood—many stories have been written about this young lady, but most are inaccurate.

Her Grandmother had no idea how much she hated Little Red. She was...so pretty, proper, popular, perky, and putrid. And the thing she disliked most was her cockeyed version of how she outsmarted the wolf. Everybody knew it wasn't true so why did they go along with it? Big Blue knew the truth. It was a wood cutter who saved her grandma, not Little Red Snot Nose.

But she realized she was losing the argument. "Okay!" she said, "I'll go with her, but I'd rather eat cold parsnips. She creeps me out, Granny, with her fancy clothes, velvet ribbons, and especially her dumb patent leather slippers that she always has to show off."

"That's gobbledygook[28]! You need to give your cousin a chance. Heaven knows you need a young friend."

Granny George decided to telephone her daughter right then to see if Little Red could go. She hooked the doorknob with her cane, pulled herself out of her rocker and clomped across the floor to the telephone. THUMP THUMP THUMP.

Before she had talked to Harriet for even a minute, however, Big Blue knew Little Red was coming. As much as she didn't like it she was going to have to put up with the little twerp[29]. But I won't let her slow me down, she promised herself, not even a little bit. And if she does I'll leave her behind and maybe the witch will get her.

---

28 Gobbledygook—nonsense, balderdash, garbage.
29 Twerp—an offensive term meaning a despicable person. Not the sound a robin makes.

CHAPTER SEVEN
Little Red Ridinghood

Snip snip snip. Little Red Ridinghood busied herself cutting out a pattern for a new gown. She could hardly wait to wear it at the Fall Fling Dance where she would be some lucky boy's date. Like her mother she was an excellent seamstress. She had won several awards in fashion design too.

As a ninth grader extra-curricular activities, such as plays, dancing, music, and singing lessons occupied much of her time. With lovely golden locks, a beautiful dimpled smile, perfect gleaming teeth, and graceful flirting manners she caught the eye of many a young lad. Her current boyfriend was Jayke Peterson, quarterback of the Pigeonpoop Pirates football team and President of the Student Council. He, too, was in the ninth grade.

"Little Red!" her mother called out from the kitchen, "guess who telephoned?"

"I don't know, Mother, I have so many friends. Was it, Penny, or Patty, or perhaps Priscilla?"

"It was Granny George, Dear. She wants you to go with Big Blue to Uncle Weirdo's castle. Her parents are in a desperate state.

"You mean they're in Wyoming with the desperados? I thought they went to Africa?"

"Oh my! Sometimes you surprise even your mother, Dear. They *are* in Africa, you silly goose, that's why the call was urgent. They're lost in a jungle, but Big Blue thinks she can help them with Uncle Weirdo's invention."

"Oh! Of course I'll go, Mother. I love Grandmother and Grandfather, and I suppose... Blue, too. But she obviously detests me."

"Nonsense! You need to give that young lady a fair chance. She has no friends...stuck way out there a hundred miles from nowhere."

"Yes, Mother, I know. I've tried to be her friend for a long time, but she's so sarcastic, and she can be mean and rude too."

"Really? She's always been polite to me. She's a bit clumsy perhaps, but with her big feet I can see why."

"Mother! Don't you remember? She used to pull my hair real hard."

"That was a long time ago, Dear, and she only did it when you called her Big Foot. Anyway Granny George needs your help. You know the way to the castle, and you're wise about Storyland. Be sure to wear your red hood and matching slippers, Dear. One should always look one's best when visiting."

⋆⇌◎⇋⋆

Little Red's mother, Harriet Ridinghood, was an attractive lady herself--with curly blond hair, pretty blue eyes, impeccable manners, and a figure like an hourglass. Harriet was not only pretty, she was smart too. Just two years after graduating as salutatorian of her high school class she was teaching natural science at the same school.

Big Blue's father, Jack Walkinghood, was a lean, medium-built, handsome gentleman of the studious type. He too was a teacher at Pigeonpoop High, teaching mathematics and astronomy[30]. Ozzie had been Harriet's steady in High School from the tenth grade on--and they were married just one year after graduating. Ozzie was in the same grade as Harriet was and he exceeded her academically by being the classes' valedictorian[31]. His special interests were astronomy and music, while his wife's interests leaned toward hiking, horseback riding, and sewing.

---

30 Mathematics and...In the late 1880's the curriculum for a typical High School included: language (reading, grammar, composition, rhetoric, English literature, Latin); mathematics (arithmetic, bookkeeping, algebra, geometry); natural science (physics, chemistry, physiology, and hygiene); geology; astronomy; physical geography; and miscellaneous (United States and English history, writing, spelling, and civil government).
31 Valedictorian vs. salutatorian—A valedictorian is a student in a graduating class who is highest in academic ranking, while a salutatorian is a student who ranked second highest.

LITTLE RED RIDINGHOOD

Little Red Ridinghood didn't have the same interests, academically, as did her parents. Even though she did well in school, her ambitions were quite different. Her dream was to have a career as a model or as a fashion designer. She was so different from her mother, in fact, some people were surprised to learn they were, indeed, mother and daughter. They could see that she was both beautiful and smart, like her mother--but unlike her mother, she seemed to always have her head in the clouds.

⋅➤══◉ ◉══◄⋅

Little Red was nervous about going to Cozy Cottage. She wanted to go, but she knew her cousin would welcome her like a fox is welcomed into a henhouse. As far back as she could remember Big Blue always bullied her and disliked everything she was interested in: like clothes, or shoes, or boys. *But, she is older now,* she thought, *and people do change.* Maybe if I'm nice to her she'll be nice to me.

Perky and excited she arrived at Cozy Cottage late that afternoon. "I'm so happy to see everyone," she announced, "and I hope I can be of assistance." Her matching dimples dipped in when she smiled her pearly white smile.

"Where are your manners, Big Blue?" Granny George scolded. "Say hi to your cousin and give her a little hug."

A *little* hug is exactly what she gave her. Then she mumbled, "Hi."

"I'm so excited about our trip," Little Red said. Then, remembering her manners, she gently tapped on the table and said, "Hi down there, Grandfather. How are you?"

His answer came back, "Noooooo, don't gooooo...don't gooooooooooooo."

"It's okay, Grandpa," Granny George said. "Don't you remember Little Red is wise about Storyland?"

"Nooooooooooooooooo she isn't."

"Don't be silly, Grandpa, of course she is."

"CROOOOOAAAAKK, isssss not!" said Grandpa.

Ignoring Grandpa's comment, Granny George turned to Little Red "It's so kind of you to come, Dear."

As if Granny George had pushed her talk button, Little Red chattered on and on, mostly about her adventure with the wolf. "I've learned my lesson about disguises," she finally concluded. "Now I know what to look for."

Big Blue wished she had stuffed cotton in her ears-- she had heard it all before.

"Do you like my new slippers, Blue?" Little Red smugly asked.

Big Blue looked. "Holy cow! You're not really wearing those are you?"

"Why yes I am, I love them."

Big Blue looked like she was going to throw up. She hasn't changed at all, she thought. She's still an airhead. One thing's for sure, she will only make the journey harder.

Little Red, in turn, peeked down at Big Blue's boots. Oh my! she thought. She's still wearing klutzy clodhoppers. She has no sense of fashion.

Early the next morning Big Blue snuck out to the woodshed, where she filled a bowl with birdseed. "Goodbye, Chippy," she whispered. "Stay safe, and don't scare Grandpa." Then she carefully hid her survival gear, including her Swiss Army Knife, under her cape, where Granny couldn't see it.

As she was about to leave Chippy stood straight up, and waiving his front paws, went, "Tk tk tk."

During breakfast Granny George gave trip instructions to Little Red, constantly reminding Big Blue that Little Red was in charge. Big Blue could barely keep her mouth shut. "Little Red has been to the castle twice," Granny reminded her, "so you need to listen to her. She knows a thing or two about Dark Forest, and Storyland."

As they left Granny George gave them a bag of muffins for their trip and wished them a safe journey. "Remember," she said, "I'll be expecting you back in two days, so don't dawdle. Big Blue, Honey, you be sure to listen to Little Red and do exactly what she says."

"Yes, Granny," she said. But she was thinking, 'I'd rather eat deer pellets'.

"I'll pray for your safety," said Granny George, "and I've made garlic garlands for you to wear."

"What?" said Little Red, "Do you expect me to wear this stinky thing?"

"Of course, Dear, It will protect you in case you run into...you know who."

"But it will make us smell awful," Little Red protested.

"That's the very idea," said Granny George.

CHAPTER EIGHT
Dark Forest

*S*kip skip skip, went Little Red, as she led the way. "First we go through Dark Forest," she said, "and then we'll be in Storyland."

Plod plod plod, went Big Blue, as she lumbered close behind--still boiling mad, and still worrying about her parents. "How far is it to Uncle Weirdo's?" she grumbled.

"Oh, it shall take us most of the day. We follow Brown Stone Path until we come to a purple and orange castle. It will be on our left."

"Oh yes!" said Big Blue. "We had better check carefully, Great Leader, we would certainly look silly going to the wrong purple and orange castle."

She's as sarcastic and mean as always, thought Little Red as she brushed away tears. I'm going to have to put up with her though, because I promised Grandmother I would teach her about Storyland. "You can be as sarcastic as you want," she said, "but I'm still going to do *my* job. Wolves, you need to know, are both clever and devious. We must be ever so cautious."

"Well, aren't you *ever so clever*," said Big Blue.

Little Red sighed. To change the subject, she asked, "Why is Grandfather so frightened of everything, Blue?

I know it was because of a curse, but Mother has never told me the details."

"Well I can guess why. She probably thought her little princess would perish if she heard the ghastly details."

"OKAY! Blue, think whatever you want, but I really do want to know."

"I'll tell you only if you'll promise to walk faster, we're going too slow. You don't seem to understand that Mother and Father are in big trouble."

"Okay, Blue, I'll go faster, I promise."

"Well, it actually happened just at the edge of Storyland. Grandpa was hunting mushrooms in Dark Forest and strayed into Storyland by mistake. Then, somehow Wicked Witch of the East found him and turned him into a frog. He stayed that way for a long time until a pretty lady kissed him and partially broke the spell. He's changed back some, but he's still terribly afraid of Storyland...and almost everything else too."

"Wow! Was that pretty lady a fairy princess?"

"Don't be ridiculous! It was Granny George, she had been looking everywhere."

"But... I don't understand. How did Grandmother know he would be a frog?"

"Duhhhh[32], she didn't. She was kissing everything: frogs, toads, turtles, even snakes. After weeks of searching she finally found the right frog."

---

32 Duhhhh—a dumb expression meaning duhhhh.

"Oh!... Thank goodness she did, I love Grandfather. I re-member the way he used to be. He was always so much fun."

"I remember too, Little Red, but it makes me so angry when I think about it. That witch nearly destroyed him."

"Is he getting better, Blue?"

"Well...maybe. He has been talking more, and he sometimes comes out from under the table--especially if anyone is talking about the castle. He loves the castle. Just before the spell he was planning to take me there."

"That would have been wonderful, Blue, I'm sorry you didn't get to go. But I'm glad to hear Grandfather is get-ting better."

"Yes, I think he is. He's still hops around a lot though. And it's awful when there's a full moon. He croaks all night."

"That's understandable, Blue. Maybe he just needs more time."

"You're probably right. But can we talk about the cas-tle now? I can't wait to see it. Does it look like the ones you see in storybooks?"

"Actually...I suppose it does. First of all, it's humon-gous. It has a drawbridge over a moat...with real alliga-tors. Inside--it's dark, damp, and dreary. There are big rooms and staircases everywhere. It has fireplaces, tur-rets, trap doors, tunnels, dungeons, and rats and bats, too. I don't know why he lives in such a dreadful place."

"Wow! It sounds fantastic. I just hope you don't spoil your pretty slippers in that *grungy* place."

"Oh, I won't, Blue. Not only am I ever so clever, I'm ever so careful too."

I can't believe her, thought Big Blue. She didn't get it. What a bimbo. She's not nearly as clever as everyone thinks she is.

Little Red was thinking too. Sometimes Big Blue is so dense. She didn't realize *I* was being sarcastic that time, just like she *always* is.

"By the way, Little Red, "is 'Weirdo' Uncle Weirdo's real name?"

"Certainly not, Blue. His real name is Charlie Humphreys. His classmates named him Weirdo because he was always blowing up things in science class. After that the name just kind of stuck."

"I was just wondering, Little Red, because he doesn't seem to mind it when people call him that."

They hurried down Brown Stone Path, gabbing about everything, but also being careful to watch for anything suspicious. What they didn't think about, however, was looking up.

Suddenly a large shadow appeared on the path. Whir rrrrrrrrrrrrrrrrrrrrrrrrrrrrrr, "Rrupppp rruppppppp," went something directly above their heads. "Criminy sakes!" said Big Blue, as she stumbled and fell.

"What the dickens was that?" asked Little Red.

"I don't know. It looks like a gigantic toad attached to a vacuum cleaner. Look, it's landing on the path."

"Rrupppppppppppp, rruppppppppppp," went... the *thing*.

As they cautiously approached the mysterious *thing*, they could see it dismounting some kind of machine. It looked like a...a...woman...? It was dressed in a... burlap potato sack, and it wore a crumpled dunce cap. Its enormous shoes looked like they were stolen from a circus clown.

It was plump, squatty, greenish, and strangely ugly. Its' huge crooked nose was covered with warts. Large earrings, shaped like frogs, dangled from its head, where there should have been ears. Its spiked green and orange hair stuck straight out, complimenting its eyes that alternated from green to red.

In a croaking voice, it...or she, said, "Hi, I'm Wendy Wi...Wi.......I mean, I'm Wendy, your...witty tour-guide. I'm here to show you the magic of Storyland. Your tour begins over here--please follow me to the yellow brick road, rruppp rruppp."

"I don't think we should," said Little Red, hanging close to Big Blue, "My friend Dorothy told me about the yellow brick road, and I..."

"You don't fool me!" Big Blue interrupted. "I know who you are. You're the one who has been flying over Cozy Cottage. You're that witch who turned Grandpa into a frog. I hate you. Granny does too. It took her forever to find him."

"Tsk tsk[33]," said the witch, "you brats are so brazen[34] now days, rruppp rruppp. So it was your Grandma who undid my spell, huh? Guess what? She's going on my Hit List. That's a shame because you *really, really* don't want to be on my Hit List. And don't think for a moment that I've given up on your grandpa, either. I'm taking Sweetiepants back, and next time I'll keep him in a cage so he can't hop away."

"YOU CAN'T HAVE HIM!" shouted Big Blue. "He belongs to us. Now back off or I'll use my magic potion on you." She didn't really have a magic potion but that was the only thing she could think of.

"Magic potion, huh! rruppppp. Just where would you get a magic potion, Brat?"

"From my Uncle Weirdo, he's a scientist and inventor, and he has a fourth degree belt in black magic."

The witch staggered back when she heard her archenemy's name. Her skin turned clammy and her eyes glared red. *Soooo*, she thought, this wretched brat is the niece of my sworn enemy--the very person who messed with my lovely looks. And now he's using his brat nieces to confront me. Hmmm, she thought, maybe I can use them to lure him away from his fortress--away from his magic potions. If I can destroy him nothing will stop me from getting Sweetiepants back.

---

33 Tsk tsk—an expression showing impatience or annoyance.
34 Brazen—boldly shameless or impudent.

"You say your Uncle gave it to you, huh? Why would he do that?"

"To protect me from ugly creatures--like you."

"Zinggggg!, Aren't you just full of compliments, Brat? That crack might just earn *you* a place on my Hit List. Say, sniff, sniff, is that garlic you're wearing? Sniff, sniff. Yes, it certainly is. Could you spare a few cloves for Wendy? I love garlic. I have a wonderful recipe for garlic-toasted butterflies that's…"

Interrupting, Little Red nervously asked, "Whaaat is that thing you were flying on? Is it just a vacuum cleaner?"

Pointing her long crooked finger in Little Red's face, the witch said, "Nooooo, Little Miss Red Hood, it's not *just a* vacuum cleaner. It's the *very best* vacuum cleaner--a Hoover-Super-Dooper-Pro-Deluxe-Turbo-Vac, in fact. It has five speeds, overdrive, cruise control, and an extra-wide seat."

What's wrong with Little Red? thought Big Blue. There she goes again, slowing us down with stupid questions. She could talk the ears off a rabbit. Can't she see the witch is a threat? Doesn't she understand how important it is for us to get to the castle? She's such a chatterbox. I almost wish the wolf had eaten her.

But she then realized she had an opportunity to destroy the witch while she was distracted by Little Red's blabbering. She reached inside her cape and removed her Swiss Army Knife. Selecting the largest blade she firmly grasped the weapon and stalked up to the evil creature, who was still talking to Little Red, and unaware of what was about to happen.

I've got to stab her in the heart, she thought, to be sure she won't recover. But as she moved forward her hand started trembling... and the rest of her body went limp. She realized she couldn't do it. Even as much as she hated the evil creature she didn't have the nerve to do the dirty deed.

But what can I do? She thought. I've got to do something. While Little Red and the witch babbled on and on about the features of the Hoover, Big Blue secretly crumbled a muffin into her handkerchief.

Finally, looking upset with herself the witch said, "Why am I wasting my time talking to the likes of you, Miss Twinkle Toes? It's Grandpa Sweetiepants I want."

Stepping forward, Big Blue shouted, "Don't you dare mess with Grandpa, or with Uncle Weirdo. If you do I will destroy you with this magic potion."

"My, my, aren't you the plucky[35] one, you cursed overgrown Brat. I should put a spell on you right now... but for private reasons I'm giving you a brief pass. I'll be back though, when you least expect me."

As she mounted her Turbo-vac she whispered, "I'll be on my way now, Brats, no need for hugs and kisses."

Whirrrrrrrrrrrrrrrrrrrrrrr, off she went, breaking off a few tree branches during her unglamorous takeoff.

---

35 Plucky—meaning brave or bold.

"Rruppp rruppp," she croaked as she disappeared into the clouds.

"Goodness gracious!" shuddered Little Red. "What a despicable creature."

"You can say that again," said Big Blue.

"Goodness gracious! What a despicable…"

"Shut up, you moron, that's not even funny."

"I hope we never see her again, Blue, she's wicked."

"She's as wicked as they come," Granny says. "But I'm afraid she *will* be back. Next time I hope I have the nerve use this."

"My Goodness, Blue. Did Granny know you brought it?"

"Well, she told me not to bring my axe, but she didn't say anything about my knife."

"I want to get away from here, Blue. I'm feeling sick."

"Yes, we need to stop lollygagging and hurry on. Promise not to tell Granny or Grandpa about the witch, Little Red. Grandpa is frightened enough already."

"I promise, Blue. I won't tell anybody. By the way, why does everybody call Grandmother, Granny *George*?"

"Duhhhhhhhh, that's short for Georgia, isn't it?"

Big Blue's answer left Little Red even more confused. "Another question, Blue. Why does everybody call Grandpa McGuire Grandpa Scaredypants? It sounds impertinent to me."

"He doesn't seem to mind, Little Red. In fact, I think he likes it. Now, I have a question. What animals live in Storyland, and are they dangerous?"

"Well, I suppose there are lions and tigers and bears. But I think there are lots more, too. I know for sure there are wolves. And from what I've read, there are also dragons and monsters. Naturally they all can be dangerous. But there are lots of silly mixed-up things too, which can be kind of fun."

Kind of fun? thought Big Blue. What is this scatterbrain talking about? Granny George always described Storyland as a scary, bad place. How could it be fun and silly? Isn't what happened to Grandpa proof it's an awful place? She decided Little Red was the *silly* one.

CHAPTER NINE

Storyland

They came out of Dark Forest into dazzling Storyland, where there were bright pretty colors everywhere. It was almost like being in a comic book. "Wow! This is exciting!" said Big Blue.

"It *is* exciting, Blue, but don't be fooled by the pretty colors. It is also a dangerous place. Funny looking things can hurt you, friendly looking things are sometimes evil, and things are not always what they appear to be."

Gee Willikers! thought Big Blue. She's full of surprises. That almost made sense.

They soon came to a curious little railroad track… and heard the faint sounds of a train, "chug chug chug," then…"I think I can I think I can I think I can."

They laughed at the silly train sounds and Little Red skipped over the tiny tracks, skip skip skip. "Come on, Blue," she said.

Big Blue haltingly stepped over--just ahead of a huge locomotive. As it hurtled by, they heard, "ALMOST GOT YOU, ALMOST GOT YOU, ALMOST GOT YOU, HA HA HA."

They stood trembling. Then, Big Blue, glaring at Little Red, said, "YOU KNEW ABOUT THE TRAIN DIDN'T YOU? YOU SNEAKY LITTLE TWIT[36]."

With her face full of tears Little Red cried, "No! I didn't, Blue. You've got to believe me. I don't want you to get hurt. I want us to be friends."

"I'm…I'm…sorry," Big Blue said. "I was just so startled." Then she added, "Do you really mean what you said? I thought you didn't like me."

"Of course I meant it, Blue. Why couldn't we be friends?"

Big Blue didn't say anything. She just stood there staring at the ground and fumbling with her belt. She desperately wanted to have a friend, but not Little Red. She would never be *that* desperate.

Little Red was still upset. "Maybe we should go back, Blue, I'm not sure we should have even started. I'm afraid something awful is going to happen."

"You're such a namby-pamby[37], Little Red. I'm going on—no matter what."

So on they went, walking side-by-side. "Have you heard about Uncle Weirdo's invention?" Little Red asked. "It's a time machine."

"Really? What does it do, put you into another time?"

"No, it tells what time it is."

---

36 Twit—meaning fool. Not a short message you send on a phone.
37 Namby pamby—lacking decisiveness.

"Then it's a clock. Doesn't he know clocks were invented a long time ago?"

"Well...he has been in that castle for a long time. And, it's more than a clock. He attached a strap to it so he can wear it on his wrist. It's pretty handy."

"Huh? Then why doesn't he call it a wrist clock? "

"Good question, you'll have to ask him."

"I wish you hadn't told me about his stupid clock with a strap. Now I wonder if he's gone bonkers. I sure hope not because I'm depending on his computeamajiggy to contact Mother and Father."

"He has not gone bonkers! Blue", said Little Red as she powdered her nose. "He's a genius. And if Uncle Weirdo says it works, it works."

"Gosh! I can't believe it. You brought a compact?"

"Of course I did, Blue, I never go anywhere without one."

On they went, now coming to a gate. "PHEW! What is that smell?" asked Little Red. "It's even worse than our garlands."

Next to the gate there stood a gigantic boot. The boot was taller than a tree and had windows on several levels. Cats were everywhere: on the rooftop, in the windows, on the gate, in the trees, and almost covering a frantic-looking man up high in the boot. With thick orange hair, pointed ears, sharp teeth, a flat nose, and long whiskers, he yelled from the top window, "Halt! Girls may not enter... meooooowwwwwwwwww."

"WE MUST!" Big Blue shouted. "It's an emergency. Just who do you think you are anyhow, you feline freak?"

"Oh what a catty remark!" he answered. It should be purrrrrrrrrrrrfectly obvious that I'm the Crazy Old Man who lives in a boot, and I have so many cats I don't know what to do, meoooowwwwwwwww." Holding his nose, he added, "Did you bring kitty litter, I hope, I hope? Wait...aren't you that silly ninny who led the wolf to her grandmother's house and almost got her eaten?........ Whatsamatter, Dearie, cat got your tongue? Meooowww-wwwwwwww."

Red with embarrassment, Little Red said, "If it's any of your business that was me, not her. Now please stop blathering and open this gate!" She stomped her little foot in disgust, but unfortunately she didn't look first. Splottttt, went her dainty slipper in a pile of fresh cat scat.

"I'll be right down," yelled the fool in the boot. "Oh, by the way, watch where you step. Meooooooooooowwww-wwwwww."

Big Blue wasn't waiting. With a mighty kick from her size twelves she sent the gate flying open. "Don't you ever talk to her like that again!" she warned.

They hurried on, happy to be leaving the wacko cat nut behind. "You were awesome," said Little Red.

"Thanks," said Big Blue. "*You* really spoke up, too."

"Well, I had to; he was up high in that boot."

They giggled and giggled about their little joke

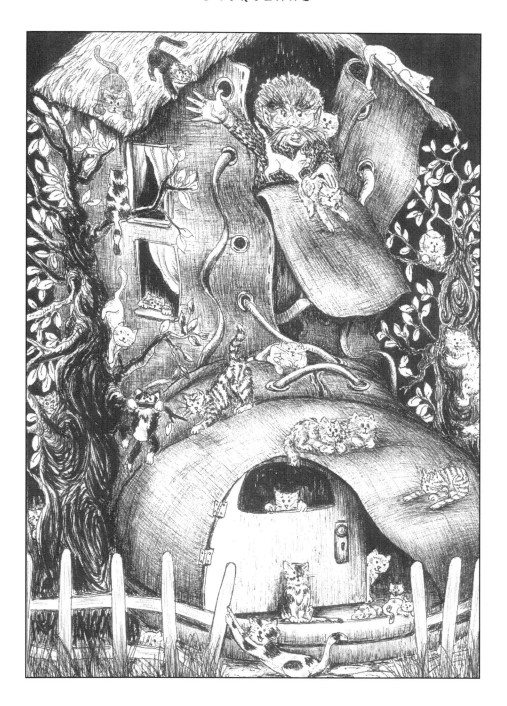

"When we come to a creek," Big Blue said, "you need to wash that slipper, it's making me gag."

Little Red was confused. I can't believe it, she thought, Big Blue just passed up an opportunity to belittle me about my foolish footwear. Maybe she's human after all.

At the same time Big Blue was wondering if Granny George might have been right about Little Red. She is nice, and she's kind of fun too. And I suppose she can't help it that she was born dimwitted.

As they rounded a corner Big Blue said, "Look! What happened to those houses? Was there a tornado?"

"No, those were the houses of three little pigs. The wolf did that."

"Oh! I read about that. Even dynamite didn't bring down the brick house, right?"

"Yes, and that shows how nasty wolves can be, Blue. You must always have your guard up."

Big Blue could hardly keep her mouth shut. Spare me, she thought. There she goes with another sappy wolf lesson.

Little Red stopped when they came to a small grassy hill. "Let's rest for just a moment on this tuffet[38], Blue, and sample Grandmother's muffins."

Big Blue agreed. But they had barely begun to eat when along came a spider. It sat down beside them and said, "Shooo! Go away."

---

38 Tuffet—a small grassy mound.

"*YOU GO AWAY!*" shouted Big Blue, "You creepy little arachnid."

"Mother!" cried the spider. "This girl with the elephant feet is picking on me."

"Ha, ha," said Big Blue. "Very funny, but I'm not falling for that one." But when she turned she found herself looking face-to-face with what had to be the biggest, hairiest, ugliest spider on the planet.

In a deep voice it said, "ARE YOU PICKING ON MY CHARLOTTE?"

"Uh...uh...uhhhh," stuttered Big Blue, as she ran away, tripping all over herself. Huffing and puffing, she finally caught up to Little Red. "Why didn't you warn me, you idiot?" she demanded.

"But I did," said Little Red. "Remember, I told you things aren't always what you think they are."

"Yes... I guess you did. I...I... just didn't believe you. Whatever, we're wasting time, let's get moving." On they went. But ahead the path divided. A rickety sign in the middle of the path pointed left, **Deture— brige out.**

"Okay, Great Leader, what now? You didn't say anything about there being a fork in the path."

"Where, Blue, I don't see it?"

"Why are you looking down, it's up ahead? Are you just pulling my leg?"

"Oh.......of course, Blue."

"Sure you were! Well, which way do we go? I have to do whatever you say."

"To be honest I don't remember the path splitting, Blue, but we should go left. We should always follow directions."

"But look how detour is spelled, Great Leader. Even bridge is spelled wrong. There's something fishy about this."

"You're suspicious of everything, Blue. Just because the person who made the sign can't spell well doesn't mean there's something wrong."

Big Blue mumbled something under her breath that didn't sound pretty, but obediently followed Little Red. She scrutinized everything, though, and didn't feel comfortable about where they were headed. Everything was changing. Soon they entered a valley that had mountains on both sides and trees everywhere. They noticed the pretty colors had disappeared and it seemed way too quiet. Big Blue was first to notice that there were bad smells. Then she noticed animal tracks. "Whoa!" she yelled. "Look at this."

Little Red looked, "Wow! Those *are* big tracks, Blue. Are they elephant tracks?"

"Don't be silly, there are no elephants here. It looks like a lizard, but it would have to be humongous. And look over here, there are human tracks...except...they are barefoot... and hairy... and look how small they are. Sniff, sniff........ They're fresh, too...but they don't smell like human footprints."

CHAPTER TEN

Dwight and the Seven Gnomes

"But, Blue," said Little Red, "if they *are* human I don't think we have to worry about them, they must be dwarfs or something."

"I'm beginning to think this is some kind of hoax, Little Red. We should go back and take the other path."

"No! Blue, we've gone this far, we might as well go on."

"Whatever! Great Leader."

They soon came to a bridge made of vines. It spanned a large river and was suspended between two huge trees. "Wow!" said Big Blue. "This is some bridge."

"It is, Blue, but I don't like it. It's too unsteady."

They hurried across, but were surprised at what they saw when they reached the other side. There were small footprints everywhere, and bicycle tracks.

"I don't remember any of this, Blue. Let's run." But as they rounded a corner the woods became even darker. Suddenly the path collapsed and they dropped into an abyss. Little Red screamed all the way down. "AHHHH-HHHHHHHHHHHHHHHHH."

Their hard landing left them bruised, frightened, and muddy. The pit was so deep they could barely see the top. "Criminey sakes!" said Big Blue. "This is a trap! It's made to catch animals."

"Oh my goodness!" said Little Red. "What if a tiger falls in...or a bear? What would we do?"

"Why are you asking me, Great Leader? *You* got us here."

They struggled to get out--but they couldn't. Finally they became so tired they fell asleep—right there in the muddy pit. But as dawn approached they heard voices.

"HELP! HELP!" Screamed Little Red.

"Ho ho!" they heard. "Looks like we bagged two of um. Damsels, too."

They looked up to see a horde of ugly little dirty faces staring down at them.

"Elves!" said Little Red. "They're elves."

"Some calls us elves, Milady, some calls us goblins, others calls us imps, a few even calls us tykes, but we're really gnomes[39]."

"Why did you trap us like we're some kind of animal?" demanded Big Blue. "Get us out of here, now!"

"Ho ho," the same one answered. "We're not particular whot we ketch, we got uses fer' all critters."

"What is that supposed to mean, you filthy pygmy?" Little Red retorted.

They soon found out. While two of the gnarly gnomes threatened them with their bows and arrows a rope

---

39 Gnomes—in folklore, small hunchbacked beings who lived in underground burrows.

ladder was lowered. After forcing their prey to climb out, the gnomes attached heavy leather straps to their ankles, and another strap, serving as a tether[40], was tied around their waists.

"Get your hands off me, you filthy beasts," whined Little Red.

"Flattery will get you nowhere, Milady," the gnome next to Big Blue said.

With a mighty blow Big Blue sucker punched him on his big ugly nose. To her amazement, her fist bounced back like she had hit a basketball.

"Oh oh!" he said, "looks like we got a feisty one, Nasty."

"Ho ho! Well, we'll just 'ave to break 'er, Goofy, that's all."

The gnomes, all seven of them, less than three feet tall each, were so hunchbacked they might have been a foot taller if they could have but straightened up. The best words to describe the lot of them would be: short, stout, ugly, and smelly. Their grotesquely large chests, arms, and hands more than made up for their short stature. Their heavy hairy legs, attached to small hairy feet only added to their Neanderthal appearance. They were ugly enough to frighten maggots away from a cow pie.

Deep dark sockets housed their beady little eyes which seemed to be extremely sensitive to daylight,

---

40 Tether—a rope or chain attached to an animal to restrict its movements.

and which registered a look of low intelligence. Their potato shaped noses and large lips were almost obliterated by thick unkempt beards. Overall, their general appearance was closer to that of an ape than a human being.

Big Blue and Little Red soon learned their names, which were easy to remember because they perfectly matched their personalities. The leader's name was Nasty, followed by Belchy, Farty, Snotty, Whiney, Goofy, and Wimpy.

The gnomes led them into a tunnel in the mountain. The tunnel was so dark they could barely see their noses, but the gnomes seemed to see everything. As they were forced deeper into the mountain it became apparent from the tables, chairs, and other things they bumped into that the gnomes lived there.

"OWWWWWWWWWWWWW, OWWWWWWW-WWWW," they heard a wailing sound, so loud it made the bowels of the cave tremble.

"Oh no!" screamed Little Red. "We're going to be murdered."

"Calm down," whispered Big Blue, "we have to stay calm so we can think."

The tunnel emerged into a large cavern which was dimly lit by gas lanterns. Just ahead they saw the source of the wailings. A large winged dragon was strapped to a treadmill and one of the gnomes was unmercifully whipping the poor creature to make it go faster. The treadmill turned a large waterwheel which drew water from a stream and deposited it onto a sluiceway. The gnomes had discovered gold in the stream and were using slave labor to mine it. In addition to the dragon, other animals were performing various tasks, all tethered and under the watchful eyes of the crafty gnomes.

They saw a pair of horses emerge from a mine shaft pulling carts loaded with dirt. Two black bears were then yanked to the carts and forced to dump the contents of the carts onto the sluiceway.

Big Blue and Little Red were then locked to a post near the treadmill. "Belchy," shouted Nasty, "Feed en' an' water em' and have em' ready fer work tomorrow."

"BRAAAAPPPPPPP," answered Belchy, "Yes sir, Boss."

Belchy brought them bowls of foul-tasting gruel and a pail of dirty water. As he left he said, "Nighty night, ladies, BRAAAAAPPPPPPP."

Little Red was so upset, so angry, so miserable, she could do nothing but sob.

"STOP IT!" Big Blue said as she shook her. We haven't got time for that, we have to find a way to escape. If we don't we'll die. Just look what they've done to that poor dragon."

SNOTTY GOOFY NASTY
WIMPY WHINEY FARTY BELCHY

"Sheeeeeeesh right," whispered the dragon, expelling only a wisp of flame. "You Kids must escape before you become too weak, like me."

"Dragons can talk?" said Big Blue.

"I can only speeeeeak for myself, Swheeeeeeeties, but I can when I want to. I just never wanted to talk to those little monsters. Oh! Please excuse my manners, my name is Dwight."

Little Red introduced herself, and Big Blue.

"You poor thing," said Big Blue. "You have scars everywhere."

"Yesssssh," said Dwight, "but worshhh than that they have broken my spiiiiirit. Death will be a relief." Dwight was carful to not directly face them when he talked, since he leaked fire whenever he said "S" words.

"Don't say that!" said Little Red. "Maybe there's a way to escape."

"Oh you swheeeeeeet Kids," he answered. "You're the first humans ever to treat me kindly. Always before humans have thrown things at me, screeeeamed at me, and even ssssshot at me. They have killed most of my clan, even my dear mother."

"Oh no! We're so sorry, Dwight," said Big Blue. "Humans can be so vicious. They're afraid of anything that's bigger than they are."

"I ssssuspect that's right," said Dwight. "What can I do to help with your esscape?

"Tell us," said Big Blue, "everything about this place, and about them."

He told them everything, starting with how he had been captured almost a year earlier. They had shot him with a tranquilizing arrow, clipped his wings, bound him, and dragged him to the work site. Every day since they had forced him to work on the treadmill, while he got weaker and weaker.

He also told them of other captives, of whom several were still working. Two human highway workers, he went on to say, were brought there a few years ago, but died shortly after that in a mine shaft accident.

As to escaping he offered a few suggestions. "They're nocturnal," he said, "ssso plan around that. When they're done with their night's work they drink ale until they're sssssstinking drunk. Then they fall asleep. Beware though, if they catch you, their punishment will be ssssevere."

"Is there another way out besides the tunnel?" asked Big Blue.

"I don't think ssso," he answered. "And watch out, they always post a ssssentry. He's often assssleep on the job though, so if you are careful you may be able to creep past him. That's all I can offer. I ssssshurrrrre hope you make it."

"We will!" said Big Blue. "We have to!

They spent the next two hours discussing escape plans, rehearsing every detail. In the distance they saw the glow of a bonfire and heard the gnomes talking, laughing, honking, belching, and farting. They silently waited. Finally, at eight o'clock in the morning things became quiet.

"Get ready," whispered Big Blue.

But just then one of the gnomes came by, checking their bindings. "I'm Wimpy," he said, "and I wish we didn't have to do this."

"Then release us," said Little Red.

"Not me!" said Wimpy, "Nasty would kill me."

After Wimpy left Big Blue removed her jackknife, which was still hidden under her cape. "He's probably on sentry duty now," she said. "I noticed the smell of rum so, hopefully, he'll soon be asleep. Be ready!"

She quietly cut the leather straps that bound her and Little Red. Then she crept over to Dwight and began cutting his straps.

"Never mind me," he said, "Savvvve yourselves. I'm too weak to go."

Big Blue continued cutting. "We're not going without you, Dwight," she said. They silently crept toward the tunnel entrance where they found Wimpy asleep on a pile of dirt. They crawled past him and ran through the dark tunnel, bumping and tripping as they raced ahead.

"Dwight, are you still there?" whispered Big Blue.

There was no answer

CLANG, CLANG, CLANG, CLANG, CLANG, CLANG.

"Oh no," cried Little Red. "I've set off an alarm."

"I'm going back to see what happened to Dwight," Said Big Blue. "Take my knife and when you reach the other side of the bridge start cutting the main vines."

"I want to stay with you, Blue."

"You must go, Little Red. Run! I'll be along soon." She bumped into Dwight at the narrowest part of the tunnel. He was stretched out blocking the passage. "Dwight!" she said, "I can't see you. How did you become invisible? They're coming. Run!"

"You are so speccccial," he said. "But please, please go. I'm too weak to go another step. Promise me if you escape you'll send help to rescue the others. Now, go! Run as fast as you can."

"I'll go only if you promise not to give up Dwight. Do you promise?"

"I promise, and dragons never break their promises."

The alarm brought the ugly crew out of their drunken stupor and into action. They quickly gathered their weapons and mounted their customized tricycles. Soon the sounds of their racing-class trykes roared through the tunnel. "RRRMMMMMM, RRRMMMMM, RRRM-MMMM." The impish gnomes were coming fast: hurtling through the dark tunnel at breakneck speeds. CRASH-HHHH!

There occurred a tremendous tangle of trykes and tykes—with Dwight at the bottom. He had changed his color to camouflage himself.

After beating the poor creature to a pulp the gnarly gnomes drove over him and sped on, hell bent to catch their prized captives.

Big Blue could hear them coming as she ran on, faster than she ever thought she could. As she crossed the bridge she was glad to see Little Red doing the job that needed to be done. She used her emergency matches to start a fire on the second vine holding the bridge. Then she gathered dry leaves and sticks to make it burn faster. The vines were so big, though, she could see there wouldn't be enough time. Just then she looked up to see them coming out of the tunnel.

"HO HO, YOU'LL PAY WHEN WE KETCH YA", yelled Nasty.

"FARRRRRRTTTTTT," added his cohort.

Big Blue grabbed the knife from Little Red and hacked away at the vine. "We can't let them cross the bridge," she said. "They'll make us slaves forever."

But the gnomes were now on the bridge, hurling out naughty words and insults.

Little Red pulled out her compact and used the mirror to reflect sunlight across the bridge into the faces of the grimy gremlins.

The blinding light was something they weren't prepared for. It caused them to crash together into a tangled heap. Then, before they could remount their three-wheelers, the bridge broke, spilling them into the river.

"What about Dwight?" asked Little Red.

"I'll tell you later, Little Red. I just hope they don't murder him."

"I do too, Blue, he's really nice."

"He' the best dragon ever."

They ran on, not stopping until they reached the fork in the road. Big Blue was so thankful for Little Red's clever use of her mirror she didn't make any additional cracks about the path she had chosen, or the fork in the road. "We made it, Little Red," she said. "Thank goodness for your compact; that was very clever."

"Thank you, Blue."

"But now we've got to make up time, we're a day behind schedule."

"Okay, Blue. But we still need to be careful. I don't like this place. Just ahead, where the path splits, is where a wolf tried to trick me a few years ago. Fortunately I was able to outsmart it."

Sure you did, thought Big Blue.......... NOT.

CHAPTER ELEVEN

Big Bad Wolf

"Owwwwwwwww," howled Big Bad Wolf. All night long he had prowled about Storyland looking for a meal. "I'm so hungry," he protested to himself, "I could eat three little pigs, and for dessert, a little red hen."

He looked about his den for something to eat, anything, even a morsel. But there was nothing. "It's hard to keep from starving these days," he grumbled. "My schemes just don't work any more, and I know why, too. It's because of those cockeyed fairytales that fill kid's heads with rubbish about wolves being bad animals. Hey, carnivals have to eat too."

"Those fairytales unfairly tip kids off to our schemes too. Now they know everything about us: what we eat, where we live, and what disguises we use. The little snots can even identify our dung. It makes me so mad my blood boils. We just don't get *any* respect! Sometimes I wish I had been born a rabbit, or a squirrel, or even a skunk—anything but a wolf."

"Owwwwwwww," he complained, "Why does everybody midjudge me? Why can't they see me for the loveable furry creature I am? Instead, they dwell on those miserable old fables."

"Like that wacky story about my visit to Grandmother's house--suggesting I was planning to eat her, and her granddaughter. Yuck! Nothing could be further from the truth. In fact I only went there to relieve her of one of her plump geese. Now isn't that something you would expect from a wolf? Hey, they don't come waddling down to our dens you know."

"Anyhow, I had barely arrived when the old lady's deranged ox of a son came barging in; screaming obscenities, and swinging a broad axe. I'm telling you, some humans act like animals. The big bonehead chased me around the cottage, hacking away at me, while his sinister mother lay in bed grinning. I jumped out of a window just ahead of a fierce blow that might have taken my head off. I won't forget that boondoggle if I live to be seventeen."

Big Bad Wolf was so discombobulated by the incident he consulted a lawyer about pressing charges against the schizoid[41] jerk. The lawyer, however, convinced him that no jury would believe a wolf over a native woodsman--backed by his failing grandmother, and her fairy-faced granddaughter.

"Owwwwww, If only I had some bacon," he mumbled, "or juicy pork chops. Mmmmmmm. One of these days I'll

41 Schizoid—an offensive term. (Don't you dare use it on anybody.)

get another shot at those piglets, especially the smart-alleky one with the brick house. When I get him it'll be payback time."

Ever since he had failed to bring down the brick house the wolf's mind had been preoccupied with wick-ed thoughts about pigs. They had humiliated him to the whole world. The newspaper headlines read, "Big Bad Wolf Outsmarted by Three Little Pigs." Some idiot even wrote a book about it. Nothing could have been more demoralizing. To relieve the pain of mortification he dwelled on devising devious endeavors to pay them back, big time. Oh what evil lurks in the disturbed brains of distraught wolves.

"*Hmmmmmm,*" he puzzled. "Just how *would* one get into a brick house, uninvited, that is? There has to be a way. *Hmmmmm,* I know! I'll be Santa Claus and come down the chimney, HO HO HO! Why wouldn't that work? Who says I don't still have it? Wait! Where would I get reindeer, or a sleigh? Fudge! Double fudge!"

"*Owwwwwwwww,*" he howled. "This moping around isn't putting food on the table. I need to pick out a cos-tume, master of disguise that I am."

In his large closet he studied his sizable wardrobe. "*Hmmmm,*" he considered, it's probably too soon to try the granny outfit again. Anyhow, I detest wearing lip-stick and carrying a purse…and I shudder at the thought of wearing a bonnet." Likewise, he rejected his turkey costume and his rabbit outfit.

After pulling out several other garments and deciding against each, he considered his sheep costume. *"Hmm-mmm.* It's a bit tattered but I can patch it up. Yup! That's what I'll do. I should practice my sheep imitation too, baaaaaaaaaa, baaaaaaaaaaa."

So he patched up the old wooly coat and brushed it as clean as he could get it. Then he looked in a mirror to be sure everything was okay. "Oh!" he said, grabbing his tooth brush, "Can't forget the pearlies. Stinky wolf-breath can be a dead giveaway."

Now dressed in his tattered costume he scurried off to Brown Stone Path to find the perfect ambush spot. His mind, like a comptometer[42], was calculating the benefits of various locations. *"Hmmmmm,* this should work nicely," he decided, as he hid in a clump of bushes. "Oh, oh," he muttered, as he wiped his chin clean of slobber. "I've got to get my mind off pigs."

Only moments later two young humans came along--chattering like squirrels. The big one was wearing a ridiculous blue-hooded outfit, and what looked like jumbo-sized army boots. The smaller one was wearing a preposterous red-hooded outfit, and outrageous slippers. Where have I seen that red ensemble before, he wondered? It's a bit like the one that bimbo was wearing at Grandmother's house a few years ago. Noooooooo...she couldn't be that dumb.

---

42 Comptometer—an early machine that performed basic math calculations.

Big Blue and Little Red were startled when a sheep jumped out in front of them. "Baaaaaaaaaaaaaaaa, my name is Bo Sheep. Where are you pretty girls headed?"

There was something about the sheep's sharp-toothed smile Big Blue didn't like. "We're going to our uncle's castle," she said. "And we don't talk to strangers."

"Why I'm going that way too," said Bo Sheep, flashing a toothy smile at Little Red. "May I join you lovely ladies?"

Little Red sheepishly blushed, but Big Blue, wary of the stranger, said, "Not by the hairs on my Granny's chinny chin chin you won't."

"Whooooa!" said Bo Sheep. "What did I do to deserve that baaaaaaaad remark?"

"Aren't you being a bit rude, Blue?" Little Red interrupted. "I don't see what harm there would be letting Bo Sheep join us."

You simpleton, thought Big Blue. You haven't learned anything. She was about to argue when she remembered Granny's instructions: *Remember to do whatever little Red Says*. So, she kept quiet and let Bo Sheep join them. She didn't like it though.

Big Blue studied Bo Sheep as they continued on. Such big sharp teeth, beady little eyes, skunky breath, and filthy coat, she thought. Then she noticed a furry tail poking through. Oh no! It's a wolf in disguise, she realized. Thinking fast she devised a plan. I can't confront him here, she thought. I need to trick him to go to the

castle. If I can get him there Uncle Weirdo will know
what to do.

With her fingers crossed behind her back she said,
"Hey, Bo Sheep, you should come to the castle. I think
you will like Uncle Weirdo's sheep."

"Sheep eh?" said Bo Sheep, drooling through his
teeth. "Yes indeed, I would relish them."

"Golly" said Little Red. "I didn't know Uncle Weirdo
has sheep."

Duhhhhhh, there she goes again, thought Big Blue.

CHAPTER TWELVE
Uncle Weirdo

In a high turret of his majestic castle Uncle Weirdo was busy filling bird feeders... and feeling sorry for himself. Blah, he thought, today will be like every other day. No one to talk to, no one to eat with... no one to do anything with--except my cranky alligators that is.

He looked down to the moat, and they looked up--with glaring, angry stares, as if to say, "Feed us, you goofy thing."

"Back off, you greedy reptiles!" he shouted. "I'll feed you right after you've been milked, and not a moment sooner." He liked having them around but sometimes they got on his nerves.

At sixty-five years old the brilliant recluse could easily have been mistaken for eighty. Living in the cold dark confines of a castle had not been kind to him. His bent frame, long arms, unkempt curly blue hair, coke bottle eyeglasses, and frazzled look would be enough to frighten most visitors away.

His blue hair came from a serious accident with electricity, which also turned his ears and nose blue. He was still strong and hard working, however, spending long hours in his laboratory. His strength was largely due to his healthy diet, which included: alligator milk, wild mushrooms, field onions, carp, newts, skinks, salamanders, razzleberries, and dandelion greens.

The renowned scientist had moved to the castle because he needed a large, secure, secret place to work on his greatest-ever project. He was confident it would be heralded as the invention of the century; so he needed complete privacy. The castle gave him everything he needed--except companionship. It left him completely isolated from those he loved. Now, with his computeamajiggy almost ready for production he found himself unbearably lonely. Most of all he missed his sister, Granny George, and, of course, Grandpa Scaredypants. He also missed his grandnieces, Big Blue and Little Red. He hadn't seen any of them for a long time.

But today as he gazed out from a high tower he saw movement on Brown Stone Path; just beyond the drawbridge. "What do we have here?" he muttered, as he excitedly grabbed his spy glass.

He saw something blue, red, and white coming his way. At first he thought it was a flag, but he adjusted the glass and looked again. Now he saw more clearly. "Yippee!" he cheered. "It looks like Big Blue and Little Red... and, a butt-ugly sheep."

He ran down the stairs and lowered the drawbridge. "Hooray!" he said. "Welcome to my castle. My alligators will be *soooo* jealous."

"Uncle Weirdo," said Little Red, "Let me introduce Bo Sheep."

"Sheep, eh," said Uncle Weirdo. "That's the sorriest looking sheep I've ever seen. But never mind that, come inside and make yourselves comfortable. I'll fetch some snail cookies and gator milk..."

"Gators are reptiles, Uncle Weirdo, they don't give milk."

"But these are Storyland gators, Big Blue, need I say more?"

"Snail cookies and gator milk, ugh! No thank you," said Little Red.

"Try them, Little Red, you will see, they are quite good, good as can be."

"Uncle Weirdo!" Big Blue interrupted, "I must talk to you right away..."

"Yes, but first let's have a snack--then we'll talk." He took them to the kitchen where he sat them on his giant toadstool chairs.

Big Blue's brain was racing. She was in a panic to send a message to her parents, but she was also worried the wolf would soon turn nasty. She had to find a way to tip her uncle off to Bo Sheep.

When he returned with the snacks Uncle Weirdo got a better look at Bo Sheep. "My, but your fleece is *not* as white as snow, Sheep."

Bo Sheep frowned and said, "Didn't you steal that line from an old story, Uncle?"

Uncle Weirdo glowered at Bo Sheep. He clearly did not like him. "My, what a big nose and sharp tongue you have, Sheep."

"Thanks, Uncle Blue Nose, I try to look my best."

"Is that so? Well you evidently weren't successful, Buttface Sheep."

"Touché[43], Uncle Blue Nose," said Bo Sheep.

While Bo Sheep and Uncle Weirdo continued exchanging jabs, Big Blue snuck around and pulled the wolf's tail out.

"Ah ha!" cried Uncle Weirdo. "A wolf in cheap clothes, eh? I'll deal with you, you ugly imposter."

Big Blue and Little Red huddled under the kitchen table as the angry adversaries battled it out.

Uncle Weirdo grabbed a butcher knife and chopped off the end of Bo Sheep's tail, tossing it out the window. "Thanks for the tip," he said. "My gators will appreciate it."

But the tricky wolf had his own plans. He toppled a chair in Uncle Weirdo's path, causing him to trip.

"Look out! Uncle Weirdo," screamed Big Blue," but she was too late. Bo Sheep hit him on the head with a frying pan.

Whammmmmm! Down went Uncle Weirdo--out cold.

Little Red began crying, "It's entirely *my* fault. I *am* just a silly ninny. Boo hoo, boo hoo."

---

43 Touché—to acknowledge a telling remark.

Big Blue knew she had to act, *now*! She hurried to the open window. "Oh look! There are the sheep."

"Sheep!" said the wolf, "where?" He ran to the window and looked out. "I see alligators, but no sheep. What is this, some sheep trick?"

"Oh no," said Big Blue. "Look straight down, next to the moat."

The hungry wolf leaned out for a better look.

Now! thought Big Blue. With a mighty kick her humungous boot connected with the wolf's tail end, SLAAAMMMM.

Out of the window flew the surprised wolf. Below, he saw nothing but water…and alligators. They grinned as he tumbled down…..down…..down, howling all the way, "Owwwwwwwwwwwwwwwwwwww."

KERSPLASH!

With their huge jaws snapping, "CHOMP CHOMP CHOMP," the alligators gave chase. The wolf's tail had only sharpened their appetite.

The terrified wolf howled, "Owwwwwwwwwww," swimming faster than a speeding bullfrog.

Little Red joined Big Blue at the window to watch the Moat Show. Then Little Red, looking alarmed, shouted, "Uncle Weirdo, are you all right?"

Uncle Weirdo was standing, but was wobbly. They ran to his side and helped him into a chair. Little Red got some ice for the bump on his head.

"Wha...wha... happened," he said. "Where is that phony sheep?"

"Don't worry about the wolf," said Little Red. "Big Blue kicked him into the moat. She is awesome!"

"She certainly is," Uncle Weirdo confirmed. Then he winked, and added, "My gators will love playing, Pin-the-tail-on-the-wolf."

Big Blue interrupted, "Uncle Weirdo, LISTEN! I NEED YOUR HELP NOW! I must send a message to my parents. They're in big trouble."

"Why didn't you say so?" asked Uncle Weirdo. "Follow me to my workshop."

CHAPTER THIRTEEN
The Computeamajiggy

In his workshop Uncle Weirdo led Big Blue and Little Red through a maze of tools, gears, gauges, gadgets, and torn-apart appliances. Whistles, bells, clocks, and chimes made noises that reminded them of middle school music class: bang bang, clang clang, dong dong, tick tick, rurrr rurr.

At the far side of the workshop he unlocked a door marked, TOP SECRET. They entered an area that was neat, clean, and quiet. "Behold!" he said, "I give you my miracle machine. It can do math, make lists, show pictures, and, of course, send and receive messages. I call it, Computeamajiggy. It's going to change the world."

"It's incredible!" said Little Red."

"I need to send a message right away, Uncle Weirdo," Big Blue pleaded. "Can you show me how?"

He invited Big Blue to sit at the console. When she pushed the START key the machine came alive. It whizzed, sputtered, and beeped. "Kick the table leg," he said. "Sometimes it needs to be booted."

"BEEP!" it went, followed by flashing lights. Finally the screen lit up. "Push this button to send an M-Mail," he said. A box appeared with the heading, M-Mail. "I'll show you about M-Mail," he said.

THE COMPUTEAMAJIGGY

"But first," Big Blue interrupted, "I need to study maps of Africa."

"No need," he said. "It's loaded with maps of the whole world. Just type in the word, 'Gobble', then type, 'Maps', then, hit 'Find'...very good! Now, in this box, type 'Canga, Africa', and then hit, 'Find'. That's it! Now we need to give it a minute to find the map you specified."

"It's awesome," said Little Red, "but how does it work?"

"It's elementary, my Dear. It transmits sound waves to the moon, where they bounce off and come back to a receiver. Big Blue's parents have my first receiver. M-Mail, as you probably guessed, is short for Moon Mail."

"My stars!" said Little Red."

Big Blue was concentrating on the screen. After three beeps, a map began to appear. "It's Africa!" she excitedly said. "And there is Canga! Now, where is Mount Killray?"

"There is the Wilde River," said Little Red. "And here is a mountain, is that it?"

"Yes! Thank you," said Big Blue. They studied the map and found the place   Jack and Jill were headed for. Now they needed to find a route to get them out.

"There are no roads near the mountain," said Little Red. "Only trails."

"But look," said Big Blue. "See the little town named Teabag. Now look at the map key. See! It indicates there is a Red Cross Station and Telegraph Office there. That's where we should send them. We just need to find a way to get them there."

117

"My Dear nieces," said Uncle Weirdo. "You're mastering this machine like it's been around forever. You youngsters catch on to new technology so fast. Keep looking. With your determination I know you'll find a way."

"I've got it!" said Big Blue. She showed how she would direct her parents to the town of Teabag.

"That looks like the best route possible," said Uncle Weirdo. "Now you need to send those directions out as an M-Mail." He showed her how to send her message.

M-MAIL MESSAGE

TO: jjwlkhd@afrjun.com

From: Unclweir@stryldcst.com

I pray you are okay. Directions will take you to a town named Teabag. It has a **Red Cross Station and Telegraph Office. From southwest base of Mount Killray, go east** *to second trail heading south. Follow trail until you come to a railroad track. Follow track east until you come to abandoned mining town. Spend first night there. Next day follow railroad track east until you come to a north-south road. Go south until you come to Teabag. Be careful! With much love, Big Blue.*

After sending her message Big Blue gave her uncle a big hug. "You're the greatest uncle ever," she said. "You will always be my superhero."

"Holy smokes!" said Uncle Weirdo. "Will I be replacing Fantastic Fred[44]?"

"Don't be ridiculous, nobody replaces Fantastic Fred. Let's just hope the message goes through."

"Hey!" said Uncle Weirdo. "Unless my memory fails me you haven't told me about your trip through Storyland. I want to hear every detail."

They told him about all of their adventures, including their encounter with Wicked Witch of the East.

When he heard about the witch his face turned red with rage, except for his blue nose and ears of course. He stomped his feet and shook his fists. "SO!" he shouted, "that old hag is still after Grandpa, huh? You may not know it but she's been trying to destroy me, too. Now she will be after you girls too, and that puts you at great risk. You're going to need something powerful to defend yourselves with for your trip back to Cozy Cottage. And you'll need to stay alert every moment. Tonight I have work to do... you'll need a secret weapon."

---

44 Fantastic Fred—early comic book hero who had great strength and claimed he could leap over small buildings.

CHAPTER FOURTEEN
The Secret Weapon

"Right after supper I'll get to work on the secret weapon," Uncle Weirdo said. "That vicious creature will certainly be watching for you."

"Uncle Weirdo," asked Little Red. "What made Wicked Witch of the East go bad? My friend Dorothy told me she was not always wicked?"

"Good question, Red. One could ask what makes any good witch go bad. Well, things started to change in her life right after high school. That's when she began hanging out with the wrong crowd. Before long she had her ears pierced and started wearing rouge. Then came billiard parlors and tight-fitting skirts. That inevitably led to roller skating on public streets, smoking cigarettes, broom-buzzing bystanders, and who knows what else. Then, from what I've heard, things got even worse after Witchcraft Academy."

"But did she always have that ugly toad look?" Big Blue asked.

"No, definitely not. She was never spectacular looking, but she wasn't ugly either......uhh. Didn't Granny tell you? I'm the one who turned her into a toad."

"You did! Wow! Tell us about it, Uncle Weirdo."

"Okay if you insist. But I'll warn you, it's a scary story."

Trembling, Little Red asked, "How scary?"

"Scary enough to bring out goose pimples on a werewolf," said Uncle Weirdo.

"Good," said Big Blue, "I love scary stories."

"It happened on a cold stormy night with lots of thunder and lightning. It was, as they say, a night unfit for man or beast. As I sat by the fireplace clipping my toenails I kept hearing strange cackling noises coming from the dungeons.

I didn't like the idea of it, but I decided I should investigate. I slowly crept down the stairs, step by step, inch by inch, carrying my secret weapon of course. My scalp tingled and I found it hard to breath. There, at the bottom of the stairs next to the moat stood true evil. Wendy Witch was pointing her wand at my gators. They seemed to be in a trance."

"It is scary," said Little Red, as she held onto Big Blue's arm.

"I yelled out, MYRTLE! STELLA! WAKE UP!" This brought them out of their stupor, but it also brought Wendy's wrath down on me."

"Well, well, if it isn't my old school chum, Charlie Weirdo," she sarcastically said. "I haven't seen you in quite a... *spell*. What are you doing here, Charlie, besides interfering, that is? I was in the process of taming these ugly creatures so they could be my pets."

"Those creatures are mine!" I yelled. "And how dare *you*, of all people, call them ugly?" Thinking back, that might not have been a wise move on my part. After all, Wendy had deluded herself into believing she was ravishingly beautiful. She must have been shocked to hear someone say otherwise. "Clever, clever, Charlie," she said, "but not especially smart." She turned her wand on me and began casting a spell, "Boogerty, braggerty, snockerty, smackerty..."

Hey, I'm not stupid. I know a spell when I hear one. Before she could complete her ridiculous chant I threw my packet of magic powder over her. It should have turned her into a toad but it only worked about half-way. Oh well, I probably didn't follow the formulary close enough. Still, half a toad is better than no toad at all."

"Jiminy cricket!" said Big Blue. "That explains why she's so crazy about Grandpa. It's because she's part toad. You know, frog and toad together ..."

"Yes, that's why that old she-devil will never give up on your grandpa. Now you see why I can't let you go back through Storyland without having a powerful weapon."

Still frightened by Uncle Weirdo's story, Little Red asked, "Whaaaathaaaapened to the witch after you thrrrewww the magic powder on her?"

"She hopped into the moat and toad-paddled away. That was the last I heard of her until last year when Granny George told me what she did to Grandpa."

"But, didddn't the alligators chase her, Uncle Weirdo?"

"No, Little Red, they were too scared. Like the Cowardly Lion from Oz, they just stood there, frozen like."

That evening they followed Uncle Weirdo to a secret passage. Down staircase after staircase they went, into the deepest bowels of the castle. The only light came from their lantern. Rats screamed and bats fluttered as they traversed down the slippery steps.

"Are you sure you want to go on?" he asked.

"I'mmmmm…okaaayy," said Little Red. "But what is that horrrrrible smell?"

"It's just bat guano," said Uncle Weirdo. "You'll get used to it."

"It is scary," said Big Blue, "but I kind of like it. Are there snakes too?"

"No! It's too nasty for snakes. Stay close now, we're almost there."

They helped him roll away a heavy boulder that hid a small door. Inside, Uncle Weirdo lit an overhead lantern that revealed the contents of the tiny chamber. There was a small table, one chair, and shelves on every wall from floor to ceiling. The shelves were overflowing with packets, tins, and jars--all with proper labels. They contained everything from Ant Juice to Zebra Powder. Mummified creatures with glassy eyes hung from ceiling hooks glaring down at them. Piles of dusty books, pamphlets, and papers filled the tabletop.

"This was the quarters of a talented wizard named Tremor the Terrible," he said. "He served the ruthless king of this castle for decades. These books and papers contain his most precious secrets. They're filled with incantations, hexes, and formulas."

"Wow!" said Big Blue. "Did you know that when you bought the castle?"

"Yes...and no. I knew that Tremor the Terrible had lived here, but I never dreamed his secrets would still be hidden here, along with his body. That was a complete surprise."

"His body? You found his body?"

"You bet I did, Red. His skeleton was sitting up in that very chair. I buried it over there--just where you're standing."

"Dooo weeee...reaaalllly have to be here?" asked Little Red, as she jumped forward. "I've never...been in such a creeeeepy place in my life."

"Sometimes I like to be scared," said Big Blue. "It makes me feel tingly all over. Uncle Weirdo," she added, "I just thought of something. Maybe we can find a formula for a potion that would cure Grandpa of his scaredyness."

"That's a wonderful thought, Big Blue, but I'm sorry to say there isn't one, not that I can find anyhow. I spent weeks searching for such a potion. If I had found one your parents wouldn't have thought it necessary to go to Africa. By the way, that tree remedy thing wasn't my idea. Your dad heard about it from that wizard in Oz."

"I know, I was there with him," said Big Blue. "What else do you know about Magnificent Wizard?"

"Well, nothing definite, but I don't trust him. I told your parents just that."

"You know what, Uncle Weirdo, I never trusted him either."

"I heard from a trusted friend that he was revealed as a charlatan[45]; that he goes from town-to-town peddling a bunch of blarney to people who are desperate for help."

"That's horrible," said Big Blue. "And if that antifear-all tree turns out to be blarney I'm going to mess with him like you wouldn't believe. I'll kick his butt into Great Black Swamp."

"I wouldn't blame you, Blue. Maybe you should kick him into the moat so Myrtle and Stella could have a play-mate. Or, maybe I could conjure up something special for him, like turning him into a white goat."

"Absolutely! Now you're talking. But isn't all this talk keeping you from making your secret weapon, Uncle Weirdo? Do you have something in mind for the witch?"

"Perhaps. I've been thinking that it might be appro-priate to make another batch of toad powder. Who knows, maybe you'll get a chance to finish the job I bungled."

"That's perfect! I'd love to finish that job. With her gone Grandpa might be cured without needing magic tree leaves."

---

45 Charlatan—a fake, someone who makes false claims.

"The recipe is in one of these books," he said. "I wish I had marked the page."

After an hour of searching through the old books Little Red said, "This may be it. It's Magic Potion Number Thirty-Four."

Uncle Weirdo examined the page. "That *is* it! Thanks to both of you for helping."

MAGIC POTION # 34 - For Turning an
Enemy into a Toad
- *Fourteen large toad warts*
- *Five bat heads (old ones work fine)*
- *Three French hens (au jus)*
- *Six gargoyle tongues*
- *One and one-half cups of slug slime*
- *Salt and pepper to taste*
- *Three-quarters cup of alligator milk*
- *Two pounds of rat droppings (fresh ones work best)*
- *Nine stink bugs*

Mash all ingredients together in a caldron and boil for two hours; while chanting: "Bright stars above, Fiery hell below...gargoyles in a pumpkin, munchkins in the snow...Evil Spirit use your powers to unload, darkness to turn this creature into a toad." Next: spread this mixture on a turtle shell to dry in the moonlight for three hours.

THE SECRET WEAPON

After reading the formula they pulled out the ingredients needed. "I believe we've found everything," said Uncle Weirdo. "Now you girls need to get a good night's sleep so you'll be sharp for your journey tomorrow. Don't worry about me--I often stay up all night. Your secret weapon will be ready in the morning. Don't forget to wash your hands and brush your teeth."

Big Blue went up the stairs first--with Little Red following close behind, grasping Big Blue's hood. "Pleeease, pleeease don't let the bats get me," she whimpered.

"You're such a wimp," said Big blue, as she boldly led the way up the dark staircase. "Eeeeeeeeeeeek, help! help!" shrieked Big Blue, "there's one in my hair."

"It's okay, Blue, it's just a moth, see, I've got it."

It took a few minutes for Big Blue to become composed enough to go on. "If you tell anybody about this, Little Red, I'll never speak to you again."

"I promise, Blue."

⋅⊱══◌◌══⊰⋅

Late that evening as he worked on his secret weapon Uncle Weirdo worried about the task that was before him. He had botched the formula the first time, but this time it had to be exactly right. His beloved grandnieces were at stake.

⋅⊱══◌◌══⊰⋅

The cousins were awakened the next morning to pleasant smells. Uncle Weirdo had prepared a breakfast of razzle-berry pancakes, salamander sausage, and gator milk. He was proud of his culinary skills.

They rushed through breakfast so they could get an early start. They dared not stay any longer because they were already a day late. Unfortunately, the telegram they were expecting from Big Blue's parents had not yet arrived.

Uncle Weirdo walked with them as far as Brown Stone Path--where he gave them a sack lunch for their trip--and the secret weapon. He asked Big Blue to carry it since she was the biggest. "Be very, very careful," he said. "An accident could turn *you* into toads."

They thanked their uncle for everything and hurried away. "I can't wait to see Granny and Grandpa," said Big Blue. Then, to Little Red, she said, "I don't think we should tell them everything. You know how Grandpa is."

"Yes," said Little Red. "I was thinking the same thing."

"I'm so excited," said Big Blue. "Mother and Father should have received my M-Mail message by now. They're probably on their way to Teabag. Things are getting better."

"I hope so, Blue. But remember what I said in Story-land, *things aren't always what you think they are.*"

CHAPTER FIFTEEN

A Cave in Africa

Jill and Jack Walkinghood, soaking wet, miserable, and angry with themselves, huddled close to a small campfire--thankful to have found shelter from the rain.

Their raft had tipped over during their river crossing-- spilling them out, along with most of their food and supplies. More importantly, they lost their maps and much of their emergency gear. As bad as things were though, they realized they were lucky to be alive--what with the river being infested with crocodiles.

After salvaging their remaining belongings, which fortunately included Uncle Weirdo's receiver, they headed toward Mount Kilray which towered above everything else some miles ahead. They blamed themselves for crossing the dangerous river. It was an impulsive deci- sion that could cost them their lives.

After reaching the mountain, however, and especially after finding a cave, they held out hope that some mira- cle would save them. Maybe, they prayed, search parties would be sent. In the meantime they realized it would be no small task to merely stay alive.

They emptied their canteens during the first few hours. "No problem," Jack said, "there's water everywhere".

When he filled their canteens with jungle water, however, he discovered a new problem. The water had a horribly foul taste: as if there were decayed dead creatures in it.

Their "Survival Kit", with its Water Purification Tablets, would have solved their dilemma, had it not been lost in the river. "We've got to have water," said Jill. "We can survive a few days without food, but not without water. There must be good water somewhere on the mountain."

So up the hill went Jack and Jill to fetch water. After locating a stream they headed back down the hill--only to be caught in a mudslide. It engulfed them and sent them tumbling head over heels. The accident left Jack with a deep cut to his forehead and Jill with a broken wrist.

After a painful hike back to the cave, Jack, minus their first-aid kit, made a cast for Jill's wrist using sticks, clay, and cloth strips torn from his undershirt.

Jack faced still another challenge when he tried to make a campfire. Only after many attempts was he successful in lighting the wet kindling. His efforts paid off though. The fire was both warming and comforting; it dried out their clothing and warmed their spirits. Jack then busied himself gathering limbs and branches, which he stacked close to the fire where they would dry out. He didn't like the thought of spending the night in the dark cold cave without a fire.

Two weeks later found them still in the same cave. It had been the most miserable two weeks of their lives.

A CAVE IN AFRICA

And on only their second day terror struck when hyenas discovered their sanctuary. From that moment on the nasty predators lingered close by, biding their time. Their insidious wailings sounded like insane laughter, "He he he he he he he he he he he."

Jack blamed himself. It was he who had insisted on going, even though the authorities had cautioned against it. The mission was completely out of character for him. Always before he had been a cautious kind of guy, avoiding activities he considered dangerous: like fishing, hiking, or basketball. Indeed, he was content with simple pleasures: like reading a book or playing the piano. Brought up in the city, he was not used to hard work, or to nature. "Why go fishing," had been his motto, "when you can buy them at the market?"

Jill, on the other hand, loved the out-of-doors, including hiking, fishing, tennis, and especially horseback riding. Together, she and Jack were an unconventional mix. "Jack," said Jill, as she surveyed their remaining gear, "what are we going to do? We're out of food, and we're almost out of firewood."

With a defeated look, Jack said, "I don't know Jill, I just don't know."

"We were crazy to have crossed that river, Jack. These monsoon rains can go on for months. There's flooding everywhere and it's getting worse by the hour."

"It's my fault Jill, I admit it. I shouldn't have listened to that miserable wizard and his self-serving story about the antifearall tree. He only told me what I wanted to hear."

"Jack, I'm not blaming you. We both messed up. But now we have to use our brains or we're not going to survive. I wish we had given more thought toward protecting our emergency gear, including our dried food."

"Yes, I agree, Jill. Big Blue tried to tell us that, remember?"

"She certainly did. Wisdom comes from the mouths of babes sometimes."

"Climbing that slippery hill wasn't smart either, Jill. Now we're both injured. And we have no way to get back across that flooded river, even if we were stupid enough to try."

"I know, Jack, and worst of all Uncle Weirdo's invention didn't work. If it had, wouldn't we have received a message by now? Surely Governor Billingsworth has been notified that we're missing; it's been fifteen days."

"Let's not be hasty, Jill. Maybe Uncle Weirdo wasn't informed about our situation right away."

"You're right, Jack, I hadn't thought the whole thing through."

But already Jacks' mind had drifted elsewhere; he was thinking about food. Even though they had carefully rationed the small amount that remained, it was all gone now. They hadn't eaten anything except a small bag of peanuts in three days. Jack had never been so hungry in his life. To ease his hunger pains he had cut off the extra portion of his leather belt, which he constantly chewed on.

He worried about their campfire too. It was the only thing that kept the hyenas from attacking. The beasts hung around the cave day and night just waiting their chances, and terrifying them with their constant wailings, "He he he he he he he." Two lions regularly came around too.

"Are you okay, Jack?" Jill asked. "You went quiet.

"Sorry, Jill, I'm just trying to figure things out. We don't have enough wood for a decent fire tonight. It's maddening, trees everywhere but hyenas keeping us cooped up here in this cave."

"Well we've got to try something, Jack. Let's tear up your undershirt and wrap it around these sticks to make torches. I'll carry a torch while you gather fire wood."

"Good idea, Jill."

They headed into the wooded area, with the hyenas following a short distance behind. Jill kept them back with her torch while Jack gathered armloads of tree branches. The torches lasted long enough for them to make three trips.

It made them feel better about their chances just having the wood stacked by the fire. "Jack," said Jill, "how many bullets are left?"

"Only six, Jill, I used too many shooting at squirrels."

"You sure did! The squirrels were in no danger, that's for sure."

"Well that was the first time I've ever fired a gun. What did you expect?"

"I'm sorry Jack. I probably should have been the one carrying it--since I did some hunting when I was young. One thing's for sure, though, we should have brought a higher caliber weapon. I doubt this thing could bring down a hyena, let alone a lion--even with two or three shots."

"I don't even want to think about that, Jill." They built a fire for the night using the last of the dry wood. Jack carefully placed the wet limbs close to the flames so they would dry out. They were determined not to let the fire go out; like it did the night before.

In the middle of the night terror had struck. "He he he he he he he," wailed the hyenas, crouching only a few feet away.

Jack and Jill awoke in a panic; to see the hideous creatures creeping straight toward them. Finally, Jack managed to get off two wild shots, which luckily, scared them off. They knew, however, it wouldn't keep them away for long.

After that they devised a plan to make sure one of them would always remain awake. The one on guard-duty would remain in a sitting position, with the gun at their side. "I'll take the first watch, Jack said. I'll wake you in two hours."

"Thanks Honey," Jill said. "Be sure to do that."

Three hours later Jack was still on guard duty, but was so weak and dizzy from hunger he couldn't think straight and his vision was blurry. An evil smell, however, caused him to look to the side, where he found himself looking eye-to-eye with a hyena. Another one stood just behind it.

It boldly stared at him--with only a tiny fire between them. Drool dripped from its lips and its huge shiny teeth reflected the fire's flames. It was measuring his every move. Jack knew it was coming.

With no time to think he instinctively jerked the pistol up and pointed it at the hyena's head. BANG! BANG! BANG!

Jill startled awake. "Good Lord!" she said, "What happened?"

"I'm sorry, Jill, I should have warned you."

After looking around, she said, "Don't be silly, Jack, I'm proud of you. You saved our lives."

"It may sound crazy, Jill, but even when it was about to attack me, all I could think about was roast beef."

Jill knew what Jack meant. "That's close enough to beef for me," she said, "I could eat a porcupine."

They roasted enough meat for several meals and ate all they could stomach. "It has a horrible wild taste," said Jack, "but I'm not sending it back." After eating his fill he fell asleep while still sitting up. Jill helped him to lie down, and he was out for the rest of the night.

"Jack," said Jill, the following morning, "wouldn't the telegram have been delivered to Mother by now? Big Blue will be so upset when it does arrive."

"Yes she will, Jill, but I know she'll be trying to help somehow. In fact, I'll bet she's at Uncle Weirdo's right now trying to contact us with his invention."

"I don't think Mother would let her go through Storyland alone, Jack, and she certainly wouldn't leave Grandpa unattended while she went with her."

"I say she'll get there somehow, Jill. I just know she will."

Jacks' right, she thought, she is strong-minded. She showed us that when we came to Africa. We almost had to nail her down to stop her from coming. Who could blame her though for wanting to help? She loves Grandpa so much...

"Jill! Jill, are you there? Or are you off in dream land? That's okay, I found it. I was looking for the knife."

She *was* somewhere else. Memories of Big Blue kept streaming back to her mind. What a strong girl Big Blue is, she thought. The bigger boys at school found that out one day when they teased her about her large feet. They only did that once.

It's just too bad her friends won't come to see her at Cozy Cottage, she thought. I feel so sorry for her. It was hard enough for her to make friends in the first place--being so big and all. And the fact that she and Little Red have never connected just makes me want to cry.

"Jill!...Jill!...Look! There's a message on the gizmo. It's from Big Blue."

"Thank God!" said Jill, as she excitedly read the message. "This is wonderful news, Jack; Big Blue's directions should take us to a little town. You were right about her; she did go to the castle."

"Yes," said Jack. "But are you well enough for such a hard journey?"

"Absolutely," answered Jill. "You're not leaving me behind with that pack of hyenas. Listen, they're laughing at us again."

"He he he he he he he he he he."

"Don't pay any attention to them, Dear, they think everything is funny."

They both enjoyed a badly needed laugh as they began making preparations for their journey out of their imprisonment. Despite their injuries they were feeling hopeful.

"We'll leave at first light tomorrow," Jack said. "It will be a grueling trip, so we must get some sleep. I'll do first watch."

⸻

The next morning found them following a trail south. The rains had mercifully slowed, but the jungle was still flooded. Only the trail was above water level. The lone hyena followed for about an hour and then dropped out of sight.

After ten hours of hard going they finally came to the abandoned mining town. Most of the buildings were in complete ruin, but the assay office[46] was in fair condition, with windows and door still in place. They were thankful to have a dry, safe place to spend the night. For dinner that evening they feasted on left-over hyena.

As Jill bit into a chunk of the charred tough meat she couldn't resist a small pun, "He's not laughing at us now, is he, Jack?"

"You're amazing Jill," said Jack. "Even with a broken wrist you can still make jokes."

"Speaking of jokes, Jack, sometimes I think this whole trip has been a joke. I'm beginning to believe the story about the antifearall tree was a hoax."

"Lately I've been thinking the same thing, Dear. I was stupid to have trusted that smooth-talking wizard. I should have listened to Uncle Weirdo, or Granny George, or to Big Blue, for that matter."

"Then...why don't we go home, Jack?"

"I'm happy we agree, Jill, I can hardly wait to leave this soggy place. I'm beginning to grow webbed-feet."

They didn't want to say it but they were far from being safe. Weary and injured, they still had another hard day ahead. Their main problem now was eating the disgusting hyena meat, finding drinkable water, and keeping their wounds from becoming infected.

"I knew Big Blue would find a way to help," said Jack. "I am so proud of her."

46 Assay office—as used here, a place where a substance (ore) is analyzed for mineral content.

"Me too, Jack, but now I feel so guilty about leaving her behind."

"She'll be alright, Jill. She's as tough as you are."

"Tougher, I think. More like Mother. Now there's a really tough bird. Yet I wonder how she's holding up while Big Blue is away?"

"Your mother is as smart as she is tough, Jill. She knew the risk, and she knows what Big Blue is capable of. Granny George will prevail."

CHAPTER SIXTEEN
Granny George

Creak crack, creak crack. Far from Africa Granny George rocked away in her old chair--waiting and fretting. She stroked her chin whiskers, stared down the path, and then stroked her chin whiskers again. Creak crack, creak crack. Her watery eyes remained fixed on Brown Stone Path.

If anything happens to those girls, she thought, I won't be able to live with myself. My old bones just couldn't take it. First I let Grandpa go to that dreadful place, and now I've done it again.

She wiped away tears and then went back to her thinking. But what else could I have done? Big Blue would have never forgiven me if I hadn't let her try to help her parents. I couldn't have forgiven myself either.

She brought her rocker to a stop and cocked her ear toward the path. With a worried look, she sighed deeply, and then began rocking again. Grandpa and I have been blessed to have Big Blue with us, she thought. She's brought sunshine to us every day, especially for Grandpa. He's definitely better since she came. In fact, it's hard to imagine how we would have gotten through the ordeal without her.

She suddenly straightened up and stared at the path. "MERCY SAKES!" she yelled. She hooked her cane over the railing and yanked herself out of her chair. She clomped into the cabin--going straight to Grandpa's table, CLUNK! CLUNK! went her cane. "WAKE UP, Grandpa!" she yelled. "They're almost here!"

"CROOOOOOOAAAAAK!" Replied Grandpa.

Like a rusty ballet dancer, she pirouetted on her toes, realigned her cane, and clomped back to the porch--choking, and weeping.

Big Blue and Little Red ran to her and gave her hugs. "What's wrong Granny?" asked Big Blue?"

"I'm just so happy to see that you made that awful journey safely," she sobbed. "You're a day late and I've been worried about you every minute. Grandpa has, too."

"Yesssssssssss," wailed Grandpa, moving part way out from under the table.

They went inside and moved Granny's rocker next to Grandpa. "Granny," said Big Blue, "You're worried about Mother and Father too, aren't you?"

"Of course I am, Honey, it's been so long."

"I know, Granny, and I'm worried too. But I did send a message to them on Uncle Weirdo's computeamajiggy... and it went through."

"What does that mean, Honey, went through?"

"That means it was received. It means Mother and Father got it. I sent them directions on how to get to a safe place."

"My stars! That is good news, Honey. I'll never doubt my brother again. Isn't that good news, Grandpa?"

"Yessssssssssssss," wailed Grandpa. "Thhhhaaaat's wooonderfulllll, CROOOAK."

"But I do need to go back to Uncle Weirdo's," said Big Blue. "I may need to send more messages. It will be much faster than telegrams. I hope Little Red can go too."

"Yes!" said Little Red. "I do want to go, if it's okay with Mother."

"We'll have to see what she says," said Granny George. "I'm quite sure, though, she'll say yes. In the meantime I want to know all about your trip through Storyland, and don't you dare leave anything out. Little Red, you can start, and then it will be Big Blue's turn."

"But first," said Big Blue, "I need to call the Sheriff. I'll tell you why when it's my turn." She made her call and told the Sheriff about the gnomes, about the highway workers, about the prisoners, and about Dwight.

Meanwhile Little Red told Granny George about their Storyland adventures, and about how Big Blue outsmarted the wolf. In spite of what Granny George said, though, she was careful to not say anything about the witch.

Grandpa came part way out from under the table so he could hear everything. He and Granny nervously listened to every word. When Little Red was done, Grandpa bravely asked, "Whaaat happened to the wolf? Did the alllllligators catch him?"

"We don't know," said Little Red. "We can only hope."

"Haaaaaaaaaaa, haaaaaaaaaaaaa, croooooaaak," said Grandpa. "Your turn, Big Blue." said Granny George, "and for Grandpa's sake, tell us all about the castle."

She did, and then said, "I love Uncle Weirdo. He's like a good friend. He's so clever. The only problem is he's terribly lonely." Then Big Blue moved even closer to her grandmother. Patting her shoulder, she said, "I have an idea, Granny. I think we should all move to the castle. Uncle Weirdo needs us, and he has lots of room. He wants us to all live together. And best of all I could invite Little Red to come for visits."

"Oh yes, I...I...would love to," said Little Red. "Perhaps I...I...could bring my friends, too. They would love the castle, and I know they would like you, Big Blue."

With tears flowing like a waterfall, Big Blue hugged Little Red with all her might. "I have been so stupid," she whispered. "You're the best friend I could ever hope for. I'm sorry I have been so awful...and so mean. If you can ever forgive me I would love to be your friend."

"And I would love to be yours," said Little Red. "I hope we can be *best* friends."

"Yes!" said Big Blue. The two cousins hugged as they had never hugged before. "Granny, isn't that wonderful?"

With a smile as wide as the Grand Canyon Granny George said, "I'm happy for both of you. I always hoped you would someday be friends. But now...getting back to that moving idea. I have to admit the castle would be an exciting place to live, and Grandpa would love it, but right now he's not ready for such a long trip. Can you imagine how many hops that would be? "

"Nooooooooo," Grandpa pleaded, "I'll goooooooooo. I love hopping."

"I'm sorry, Grandpa," Granny said, "It just wouldn't work."

It was time for Little Red to leave but she would be coming back in just two days for the return trip to Uncle Weirdo's. "I can hardly wait," she said.

⊷⊜ ⊜⊶

Big Blue was extra busy during those two days. She did all her chores, and in between, made several private telephone calls. Granny George was curious about who she was talking to, and why she was whispering. *She's probably talking to Little Red,* she decided. But she wondered what foolishness they were up to?

Two days later Big Blue anxiously waited at the door for Little Red's return. When she arrived they hugged, and whispered, and giggled... and giggled.

"WHAT'S GOING ON OUT THERE, GIRLS?" Granny George shouted. She pulled herself out of her rocker and hurried to the door, THUMP THUMP THUMP. With an astonished look, she said, "What are the horse and carriage for? What's going on?"

"You'll see!" said Big Blue. "Please trust me, Granny, I have a plan. We're *all* going to the castle."

"Not all of us," said Granny George.

"Please listen to my plan, Granny," Big Blue said. Then she told her everything, right down to what the horse and carriage were for.

"Well it all sounds great, Honey, but let's see what Grandpa thinks."

"Yessssss," wailed Grandpa, as he hopped around like a frog.

"Well then, we need to get packing so we can leave first thing in the morning."

"Yipeeeeeee," said Grandpa, "CROAAK."

Big Blue was overjoyed that Granny agreed to her plan. Secretly though, she was worried about what plans the witch might have.

CHAPTER SEVENTEEN

Back Through Storyland

Click clack, click clack, went Betsy's hooves on the hard stones. Granny George sat up front driving, while Big Blue and Little Red kept company with Grandpa.

The table, with its long tablecloth, had been placed in the center as Grandpa dictated. They were pleased that he wanted to go, even though he insisted on wearing goggles, a crash helmet, and taking his teddy bear.

Big Blue, with her grandmother's permission, had placed her axe in the back of the carriage where it would be easily accessible. And she remembered to bring her friend Chippy along. She thought he would love the castle.

As they entered Storyland Granny George pulled her bonnet down low to shield her eyes from the brightness. Then, as they approached a railroad crossing she pulled Betsy to a stop, "Whoaaa, Betsy," she said. "Girls, is this where you were almost hit by that spiteful train?"

Just then they heard train sounds...chug chug chug.

"HURRY ACROSS, Granny!" Little Red screamed.

Granny urged the old mare on and they dashed over the tracks...just as the giant train roared by, "ALMOST GOTCHYA! ALMOST GOTCHYA! HA HA HA. "

Big Blue reminded Grandpa about the wicked train. "After it almost hit us, Grandpa, the evil thing laughed at us."

He pulled the tablecloth up to have a look for himself. As it roared by, he shook his long finger at it and shouted, "Shaamme, trrraaainnn!"

"It looks like Storyland is as funky as ever," Granny George complained. "Why President Cleveland doesn't do something about places like that I'll never know."

On they went, now bouncing onto a bumpy bridge over a bubbling brook. Their cart went, bump bump bump. A gruff-sounding voice roared out from below, "WHAT BUM IS BUMPING ON MY BRIDGE?"

Granny George yelled back, "SHUT UP! You grumpy old goat."

A hideous creature jumped out. It trip trapped to the cart. "GIMME TWO PENCE, AND BE GONE!" it roared.

Little Red held her nose. The creature's scent was even worse than a gingerbread man she once met whom everyone called, The Stinky Cheese Man.

"This is nothing but highway robbery!" Granny George complained. But she paid the toll, saying, "You're the ugliest troll[47] I've ever paid a two pence troll toll to."

They were surprised to hear Grandpa giggling under the table, "Hee hee hee."

---

47 Troll—a mythical, ugly, supernatural being that lives in dark places and is hostile in nature. Modern day trolls are often referred to as Grandpas.

"You're right, Granny," said Big Blue, "this trip is turning out to be as crazy as the first one; I just hope it doesn't get worse."

But only a short time later Granny George shouted: "Look, The Three Bears[48]!"

There they were, holding bowls in their paws. Papa Bear hefted a large-sized bowl of *Goat Meal*. Mama Bear's medium-sized bowl was full of *Corn Chicks*. Baby Bear's wee-sized bowl contained *Cocoa Pups*. The Three Bears smiled and waved.

They waved back, excited to see The Three Bears in person. Grandpa, and his teddy bear, came all the way out from under the table for a closer look.

"Humph!" Granny George said. "When I was young Storyland bears all ate porridge." With that, she giddy-upped old Betsy. "We need to make up lost time if we're to get there before dark," she warned.

When they came to The Crazy Old Man Who Lives in a Boot they found him to be friendlier this time. When he saw Big Blue he rushed to open the gate. "Welcome," he said, with a catty smile. "I recognized your boots from a mile away. Say! Wouldn't you like to take a kitty home with you, or two, or three...or more, meowwwwww?"

"No," said Little Red, "but we do have something for you." She and Big Blue heaved out a bag of kitty litter. "I hope this helps."

---

48 The Three Bears—the baby from this famous family became a star player on a Chicago football team.

"It certainly couldn't hurt... meowwwww".

They all laughed, even Grandpa Scaredypants, and that was something of a record. Grandpa had laughed twice in the same day.

Granny George, still chuckling, said, "What other craziness could we possibly run into?" Her words were barely out of her mouth when they came to an orange and black ribbon across the path. A sign in the middle read, *THE FINISH LINE.*

"Are we in Finland?" asked Little Red.

"Duhhhh!" said Big Blue. "I'm going to pretend you didn't say that."

As Big Blue and Little Red stepped out to see what was going on they were mystified by the strange noise that was coming their way, Herrrrrrrr, brrrumm, brrrumm, herrrrrrrr. There was a cloud of dust too. They ducked for safety behind the carriage--just as a motorized bicy-cle--piloted by a grinning green and brown thing came roaring through the ribbon. Betsy jumped; nearly upset-ting the carriage.

Big Blue ran to help Granny George back into her seat, and to soothe old Betsy. "It's just some lunatic, Granny," she said. "Are you all right?"

"Yes," she answered. "But I'd like to take the whip to that driver."

"My goodness!" Little Red screamed at the green and brown thing. "You almost ran us over, you little...you lit-tle...whatever you are."

Taking off gloves, helmet, and goggles, the green and brown thing said, "I'm weally, weally sorry, Waidy. I'm pleased to meet you. My name is Willard Turtle."

"What on earth is a twurtle doing dwiving...I mean... a turtle...doing...driving that thing?" asked Little Red.

"Well," said Willard, "Wen you're a wittle turtle, you need to use some twicks. You see, that was a wace between me and that wascally wabbit, and he can weally wun fast."

Just then a dust cloud came across the finish line. When the dust settled, a dirt-covered rabbit appeared. With a disgusted look, it yelled, "You cheated again, you creepy little tortoise. Shame on you! You always cheat."

"Ha ha, Wabbit," said Willard. "I wunn again. Better luck next time, Wabbit."

"But, Wabbit was wight," said Little Red. "... I...I... mean..."

"Never mind!" interrupted Granny George, as she beckoned for Big Blue and Little Red to get back into the carriage. "That's about enough foolishness for a lifetime."

"Now I see what you mean, Little Red, about Story-land being *kind of fun,*" said Big Blue.

As they started ahead, Grandpa poked his hand out from the cart to give Willard a high five. "Turtle Power!" he said.

Now the castle was only minutes away and they were getting really excited. Big Blue looked worried, though. "Little Red," she whispered, "I want you to have half of my magic powder. I have a creepy feeling about things."

154

CHAPTER EIGHTEEN

Wicked Witch of the East

In her sub-earthen house built into a hillside Wendy Witch busied herself with her daily routines. Picking out what to wear was an easy task, since her dresses were all made from burlap. It was her next routine--picking her nose--that was not so easy, as any toad will confirm. As she picked away with her clumsy webbed fingers she mused, "When will somebody invent a mechanical gadget to make this easier?"

At this point in her life Wendy was a most unhappy witch. With her advancing age she had come to realize that witchcraftery is not all that it's cracked up to be. Sure, it's glamorous and exciting work when you're young, but all that becomes old hat after a few decades. Now, she was not as pretty and popular as she once was. Indeed, when she was in Witchcraft Academy she had lots of suitors. Those were the good old days.

But now a sore sight for eyes she had no suitors, no friends, no visitors, nobody. Even her pets had decided they were better off dead. All that was left for her now were memories. Herman Waters was one of those memories. "Herman My Honey," she cried out as she hugged her large fruit jar, "Why did you do it? You were beautiful as a frog. We could have had a wonderful life together."

Charlie Weirdo was another memory—but not a good one. "Your time will come, Charlie," she threatened. "I might have had a career in Hollydazzle, like my sister, but for you. No one puts a curse on Wendy and gets away with it."

But her favorite memory of all was of Grandpa Scaredypants, or as she called him, Sweetieypants. She was infatuated with him and determined to get him back...and woe to anybody who might stand in her way. Still on her morning routine Wendy unloaded flies and bugs from her insect zappers. That should be enough for now, she thought; I must watch my figure.

After breakfast, as usual, she performed her pre-flight safety inspection. She checked each piece of equipment on her Turbo-Vac, shouting out her findings as if there was someone there to hear them. Being a true *creature* of habit, she followed the same routine she had been taught years ago at Vacuum Cleaner Flying School. "Power unit—CHECK! Lights—CHECK! Speed control— CHECK! Bug spray—CHECK! ALL FUNCTIONS OP- ERATIONAL AND READY, SIR!" she smugly reported.

She was proud of her magnificent machine, as well as she should have been. She worked hard to keep it clean and in perfect working order. When she was young, like so many youngsters, she did reckless things: like buzz- bombing bystanders, driving with one hand, and not buckling her seat belts. But she learned her lesson about safety after a bad crash and a couple of close calls. Now, safety was of the utmost importance.

Let's see, she pondered, today is Friday, so it's time to patrol Brown Stone Path from Billy Goat Bridge to Weirdo's Castle. Who knows what unlucky traveler I might encounter, rruppppp? I'd love to catch Charlie Weirdo away from the safety of his castle. I might even run into Grandpa Sweetiepants. He can't hide forever.

Her patrol preparations didn't stop her from thinking about Grandpa. Yes! Grandpa, she thought, you're the one. I've got to get you back before I'm too old to croak. Remember the beautiful music we made together Sweetiepants: rrupp rrupp rrupp---- ribbit---- rrupp rrupp rrupp----ribbit. It was Frog and Toad Together.

She sneered as she remembered her encounter with Big Blue and Little Red.If those menacing snot-nosed brats get in my way again they'll be sorry. I'll turn them into mice and sic a cat on them.

She cleaned her goggles, tucked in some sagging warts, tightened her chin strap, and mounted her trusty Turbo-Vac. Click, click, went her seat belts. Whirrrrrrrrrrrrrrr, off she went, "Rruppp rruppp."

She flew her machine up, up, up, until she was just below cloud level. At that altitude she could see great distances, but was still above bird level. Bird collisions were her greatest fear. Her worst accident had involved a head-on collision with a turkey buzzard. She survived the crash but her snout had been permanently distorted. She took some comfort, however, in knowing the buzzard fared even worse.

"Looky looky," she mumbled to herself, as she saw movement on Brown Stone Path. She slowly circled down, down, down, for a better look. "Ah ha!" she croaked. "It's Granny George and the snotty brats. But Grandpa Sweetiepants isn't with them, unless...he's hiding under the table."

⋅⊸══◉ ◉══⊸⋅

Now very near the castle Granny George was having problems with Betsy, who abruptly stopped and refused to go on. "What's ailing you, Old Girl?" she yelled. "Giddy up! Suddenly the trees began shaking, and the leaves quaking, and they heard a disturbing unnatural sound overhead. Whirrrrrrrrrrrrrrrrrrrrrrrrrrr, "Rrupppppp, rrupppppp."

Betsy reared up, tipping them out of the carriage.

"Rruppp, rruppp," croaked Wendy, as she circled down for her landing. "I've got you now, Sweetiepants, remember me?"

Grandpa leaped under the table, "Noooooooooooo," he moaned.

After landing her craft the witch stood over Grandpa. "Hide under the table; marry before you're able, rruppp

rruppp." She pointed her wand at Grandpa. "It won't hurt a bit, Sweetiepants. Be a big boy."

"Bigga-de-bo, bigga-de-ba, I cast this spell on Grandpa.

Doodle-de-da, doddle-de-deedie, let him be my little sweetie.

Piddle-de-peede, piddle-de-pog, turn him into a..."

"STOP!" screamed Big Blue, "or I'll destroy you with my magic powder."

"Ha!" said the witch. "If you had magic powder you would have used it before, Brat."

The thought of the witch messing with Grandpa enraged Big Blue. She knew she had to destroy her...now. She opened the secret weapon and ran forward, but on the way tripped on her bootlace. Flopppp, she fell to the ground--spilling the powder .Oh no! she thought. I've botched everything. I'm such a klutz.

"Rrupp," croaked the witch "You missed me, you missed me, now Grandpa has to kiss me."

The witch, preoccupied with Big Blue's predicament, had no idea what was going on behind her back. From the left Little Red was approaching fast, carrying the secret weapon. From the right Granny George was coming too, although not so fast, carrying Big Blue's axe. Little Red got there first. Suddenly the witch realized she was being sprinkled with powder.

"You wretched wrench!" she croaked.

"Don't you mean winch?" asked Little Red.

"The word is, wench[49]! you idiots," Big Blue corrected.

The witch turned and pointed her wand at Little Red. "Tweety ti...tweeti... rrupp, rrupp." She was shrinking, shrinking, shrinking. Her fingers and toes became completely webbed. Her cheeks became enormous, and huge warts appeared everywhere. Hopping mad, she said, "You Brats are going on my list, rrruppppppp."

Actually she looked about the same, only much shorter and not quite as ugly.

"Thunderation!" said Granny George. "You've saved us, Little Red. Where did you get the magic powder?"

"Big Blue gave it to me...Whoops! I let the cat out, didn't I, Big Blue?"

Big Blue picked herself up and ran to hug Little Red. "I'm so proud of you, Little Red," she cried. "You were awesome."

"It's obvious there are things going on here I don't know about," said Granny George. "Maybe it's best I don't."

Big Blue, singlehandedly, tipped the carriage upright and they continued on. As they moved ahead she looked back to see the ugly harpy boldly staring at her. It made Big Blue cringe with fear to see her look that said, *"I'm not done with you!"*

---

49 Wrench, winch, wench—these words are easily confused. A wrench is a tool to turn nuts, a winch is a pulley devise, and a wench is a wicked young lady. Granny George taught the meanings this way: "Waynard Weevilnose used a winch to retrieve the wrench the naughty wench threw into the well."

With the witch out of sight Granny's spirits improved and she began singing, "Hooray! Hooray! The witch is gone, the witch is gone, oh what a happy, happy day."

"Gooood ridddddanccce wiiittttcchh," Grandpa chimed in.

"Tell me, Little Red," asked Granny George, "why did the magic powder change the witch to a toad? Why not a snake, or something else?"

"Uncle Weirdo could probably tell you best," said Little Red. "But I do know that the magic powder...uh......like actually probably helped her to become what she nearly already really was--almost."

"Gibberish!" Granny George said, wondering what on earth she was talking about. At that, she grabbed the reigns, "Giddy up, Betsy," she said.

As they traveled on Granny George began stroking her chin whiskers--which meant she was thinking. "Someday," she said, "when Grandpa remembers more about that she devil he will have quite a story to tell."

CHAPTER NINETEEN
Grandpa's Story

In his safe-place beneath the table Grandpa heard everything, including the talk about the witch. But with her gone he was not nearly as frightened. Indeed, he was feeling better all over, and transforming faster too.

How could he tell his story, he wondered, when there was a big part of it he couldn't remember? Now he wanted to remember. He didn't feel whole with a piece of his life being a mystery. But all he could recall about the witch was that she somehow was responsible for him becoming a frog.

As he reminisced it occurred to him that his brain had remained human even when he was a frog. Even though he looked like a frog, croaked like a frog, and jumped like a frog, his thinking had stayed human. Now just the idea of it made him shudder.

"Grandpa's shaking again," Granny hollered. "I can feel it clear up here. Try holding hands with him, it makes him feel safe."

Soon Grandpa settled down and was thinking again. He reasoned that he might get over his scare-dyness if he forced himself to remember that horrible day in Storyland. But the more he thought about the witch the more frightened he became. "Ohhhhhhhhh," he moaned.

Clenching his teddy bear helped, and he soon went back to his thoughts. There must be another way to do this, he concluded. Maybe I should try to remember other things first, happy things. Then I'll think forward until I'm up to date.

He let his mind wander back to happier times. He remembered how he liked tending his beehives and collecting honey. His bees produced the most delicious honey in the world, and year after year won first place at Pigeon-poop County Fair.

Then his mind swerved to a scene on the river. It was a beautiful day and he and Granny had gone fishing. She brought a picnic lunch so they could spend the whole day together catching catfish and enjoying her cooking.

Grandpa was broadly smiling now as the carriage clamored on. He was remembering Big Blue's summer visits. He and Big Blue got along together like puppies in a box. She loved the outdoors as much as he did, and she wanted to learn about so many things: such as fishing, survival, tracking animals, building a campfire, and a hundred other things.

Little Red sometimes visited too, he recalled, but never the same time as Big Blue. Little Red preferred things like playing Parcheesi, skipping rope, and hearing him tell tall tales. She liked to help her grandmother in the kitchen too, making sourdough bread and gingerbread cookies. What a lucky grandfather he was, he realized, to have such wonderful granddaughters.

But now his thoughts turned to a day when he was walking in the woods searching for spring mushrooms. This time he had gone further into the woods than ever before. Indeed, he had strayed beyond Deep Forest into Storyland.

He remembered how excited he was when he found some choice mushrooms. As he gathered them, however, he had a creeping feeling he wasn't alone. He looked up and was amazed to see a house only a few yards away.

He recalled how uneasy he felt about trespassing on someone's property. The house, he noted, was made of sticks, stones, and mud, and built into the side of a hill. It was surrounded by trees and bushes, making it almost invisible.

Who would live in the middle of the woods, he pondered, where there are no roads? How would they get back and forth? What a strange house it is, too. It's so low you couldn't even stand up. Then he noticed a puff of smoke coming from the chimney.

What happened next about made him dirty his pants. "Rruppp rruppp," went something close behind him.

"Noooooooooo," groaned Grandpa, from under the table. He was remembering the bad part now. It was all coming back. But with his granddaughters holding his hands he found the courage to go on; to recall the details of what was the scariest event in his whole life.

He turned to face the strange croaking sounds--ready to defend himself with a rock he had picked up. What he saw next both shocked and puzzled him. What was it? Was it an oversized toad, or an unearthly looking squatty woman? Before he could say anything, however, it said "It's not polite to stare, Sweetiepants, haven't you ever seen a pretty lady?"

Try as he would Grandpa couldn't remember his exact words, but they were something like, "I'm pleased to meet you…Miss, but I must be on my way."

On the other hand, he did remember her curt reply. "Not so fast, Sweetiepants.   It's impolite to call on someone without making time for tea and biscuits. Do come inside and sit for a …*spell*… rruppp rruppp."

At that point he realized she must be a witch. He recalled running away--faster than most octogenarians. But he was tripped by a rope which magically flew through the air, entwining his legs.

He looked up to see the ugly harpy standing over him. "Rruppp rruppp, playing hard to get, huh?" she croaked. She pointed her silvery stick at him and began chanting some strange poem. It went something like, bigga-de-bo, bigga-de-ba."

"Ohhhhhhhhhhhhhhh," wailed Grandpa, trembling all over. Big Blue lifted the tablecloth and offered him some fried grasshoppers. It helped to calm him.

Soon he was thinking again. He realized the witch had cast a spell on him and was keeping him captive in her house. He remembered trying to find a way to escape.

He recalled how she toyed with him for weeks, not allowing him water or food unless he did exactly what she wanted him to do. When she said, "jump," he had to jump or he wasn't fed. She also forced him to sing boring frog and toad songs: "Froggie went walking on a summer's day, a-hum-de-ee, a-hum-de-ee..." He hated it! She made him play silly games, too, like hopscotch and leapfrog. And when she did feed him, it was always the same thing, flies and bugs.

Once when she was napping he hopped up on the counter, looking for food. He was shocked to see an over-sized frog in a huge bottle. Even though it was obviously a frog its head looked human. It had been pickled and placed in a pretty bottle with a label that said, HERMAN MY HONEY.

Now he remembered his great escape. One morning she had left the door ajar[50] when she came in with firewood. He had been hiding behind a broom waiting for just such an opportunity. Out he hopped as quickly as a rabbit.

---

50 Ajar—meaning partly open. Or, a good container for bugs and crickets.

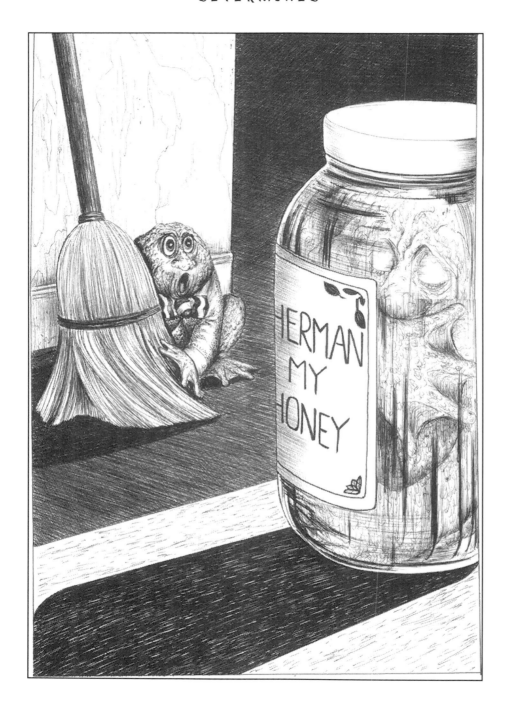

GRANDPA'S STORY

He soon found however, much to his horror, that the outdoors is a dangerous place for a human-brained frog. He didn't know what frogs do. He didn't realize that he was now prey for hungry predators[51]. He couldn't even jump straight. He had gone only a short distance when he saw a moving shadow on the ground, and alertly realized it wasn't his. He quickly jumped into a hollow log and looked back to see a hawk flying away. At that point he understood what it feels like to have predators wanting to eat you.

Then, just as he was about to hop out from the log he heard the witch calling out, "Sweeieypants, where are you, Naughty Boy? I've got a treat for you".

He stayed glued to his hiding place. Even when she jammed a stick into his nose he somehow managed not to croak. "Sweetiepants," she called as she scuffled away, "Wendy misses you."

He remembered being so frightened he wet himself. That's when he realized he needed to find a better hiding place. After first checking for predators he hopped down the path. He was surprised at how far he could jump--for a beginner. Hop, hop, hop, he went, determined to hop all the way back to Cozy Cottage.

But his hoppy mood quickly changed when he saw a black cat racing toward him. "CROOOOOAK," he

---

51 Prey vs. predator—prey is an animal hunted for food, while predator is an animal that hunts other animals for food. Here's how to remember the difference: the prey prays the predator doesn't pounce on it.

belched. What was he to do? Knowing that cats don't like water, he made a long jump...that took him into a pond. SPLASH!

There, he found himself surrounded by lily pads, which he soon decided was a good thing. The pads prevented predators, like hawks, from seeing him from above, and the stems acted like a barrier around him.

A bit later the stems proved their worth. A big-mouthed bass appeared nearby and eyed him with a hungry look. But despite several rushes at him it couldn't get through the stems. It terrified him! Also, the witch came around every day searching for him. Once she parted the lily pads only a few feet away. He was so frightened he stayed put for three days without anything to eat. He had about given up all hope of surviving.

A bump in the path brought Grandpa out of his thoughts and made him realize he was still under the table--not under lily pads. He peeked out at the path, wondering how much further it would be.

"We're almost there, Grandpa," said Big Blue. "How are you doing?"

"Betttttttter," he answered."

"Good! Don't worry about anything, Grandpa, everything's going to be okay."

He was soon thinking again. He smiled as he remembered the day Granny George rescued him. He had been hiding under the lily pads for four days when he heard her calling out, "GRANDPA! GRANDPA!"

He remembered how excited he was to hear her voice. Without first checking for predators he boldly jumped onto the path.

"Whoa!" she said, almost stepping on him.

Forgetting his limited vocabulary, he said, "RIBBIT, RIBBIT, RIBBIT."

To his amazement she picked him up and gazed into his eyes. "GRANDPA! she yelled. Then she kissed him right on his big slippery lips. But then she dropped him, and with a disgusted look she shook pee from her hands.

He felt terrible, but he couldn't help it. That's what frogs do when they become frightened...or excited.

The tablecloth went up a bit and Big Blue peeked in. "We're getting really close now, Grandpa."

"Grandpa," Granny called, "Now that the witch is gone are you feeling better?"

"I'm much better," he answered.

"That's just great Grandpa. You'll be happy to know the castle is just ahead."

They stopped on the drawbridge so Grandpa could see the alligators. He came out from under the table for a long look. This time he wasn't wearing his goggles or crash helmet, and he had left Teddy behind.

CHAPTER TWENTY
The Castle

From a turret high in his castle Uncle Weirdo saw them coming. Trembling with excitement, he yelled, "Yippeeeee!" He was as nervous as an Eagle Scout without matches, and at the same time as happy as a pig in a puddle. When he lowered the drawbridge a large banner came into view: WELCOME TO THE CASTLE.

As they entered, the old fortress lit up like a Christmas tree. It had never before witnessed such a joyful reunion. The castle was magically transformed from a dreary dark stronghold to a warm and friendly home.

Uncle Weirdo had worked hard to make them welcome. In the turrets he had prepared rooms for everyone. He even had an extra bed in Big Blue's room for Little Red to use whenever she visited. Everywhere everything had been scrubbed and made ready.

After exchanging greetings they all gathered in the great parlor around the fireplace. "I'm so happy to see everyone," Uncle Weirdo said with tears in his eyes. "Big Blue told me to plan on your coming and she delivered."

WELCOME TO THE CASTLE

"Big Blue can be very persuasive," said Granny George. "And we couldn't have held Grandpa back with a bowl of grasshoppers. I'm so glad he did come, actually, because getting out of the cottage has solved his problem. He's transforming so fast now it's hard to keep him in clothes that fit."

"That's right," said Grandpa, who was sitting in a real chair.

"Beneath those warts," Uncle Weirdo said, "I'm beginning to see the Grandpa I used to know. And with Wicked Witch gone the curse will fade away much faster. Soon you'll be back to your normal self, my old friend."

"Oh, that will be so wonderful," said Granny George. "This would a perfect day if only...if only..." Granny began crying and couldn't stop.

Big Blue helped her into a chair. Uncle Weirdo volunteered to make a pot of hot cocoa. "Granny," said Big Blue, "everything is going to be all right. I know my message went through, and I'll bet they have already found their way out of the jungle."

"You're right, Honey; I need to buckle up and think positive."

"N-e-s-t-l-e-s, nestles makes the very best...chocolate" sang Uncle Weirdo, as he arrived with a tray loaded with mugs of the hot beverage. "I propose a toast to Grandpa's recovery. It's wonderful to have you back, Grandpa."

"Crooo........ thank you," said Grandpa.

After the toast Uncle Weirdo took them to the dining room and announced: "You are invited to partake of my surprise meal."

"Nothing you do surprises me," said Granny George.

"Here's how a surprise meal works," he said. "As I serve each course, we'll see who can correctly guess the ingredients. There's a prize for each winner. Here is course number one," he said, as he filled their bowls with a steaming-hot, thick, lumpy liquid--greenish-brown in color, and with small black pellets.

After tasting a spoonful Little Red ventured, "Is it spinach with black beans?"

"Not even close," said Uncle Weirdo.

Laughing, Granny George guessed, "Is it ground up weasels, with crow's toes?"

"Much closer," said Uncle Weirdo. "But still not correct."

They enjoyed playing the game through three more courses without a single correct guess. "Dessert is your last chance," Uncle Weirdo warned. "See if you can guess what this is?"

"I know, I know," said Big Blue, "That's gator milk, and those are snail cookies."

"Bingo! The young lady wins," he announced as he gave her a prize.

"I'm almost afraid to open it," she said as she ripped open the package. "What is it?" she asked?

"Why it's a mechanical nose picker of course. I invented it."

"But I don't pick my nose! Uncle Weirdo," Big Blue protested.

"Balderdash! Everybody picks their noses."

After finishing Uncle Weirdo's memorable meal they retired to the parlor, where they spent an enjoyable evening catching up on things, and seeing Uncle Weirdo's newest inventions.

"Here's something handy," he said. "I call it a popup-breadmajiggy. You put a slice of bread into this slot, push down on this lever, turn the knob to either jelly or peanut butter, let's do jelly, and in only a few minutes, up pops your bread, only toasty like, and with jelly."

He loaded the machine, and they waited...and waited...and waited.

BAMMMMM, up shot the bread. Higher and higher it arose.

They cheered as it soared to the castle ceiling.

Down...down...down, came the toast...and jelly, raining all over them.

As they laughed hilariously, Granny George said, "You're simply a genius, Dear Brother, a genuine genius."

"Wait! I have another invention you haven't seen. It's in the dungeon. I've invented the world's first gator milking machine. I'm thinking of calling it Gator Maid, or... possibly, Monster Milker."

"Whooooa!" said Granny George. "Maybe some other time, Uncle Weirdo. I don't think we're ready for that tonight."

With a quizzical look Big Blue said, "Speaking of alligators, Uncle Weirdo, we heard 'tick, tick, ticking' sounds coming from the moat. What was that?"

"That, I hate to say, was my time machine with a strap. It fell off my wrist while I was milking Myrtle and the cursed beast ate it."

"Oh brother!" Said Big Blue, with an alarmed look. "I'm sorry I asked."

"RING, RING, RING," went a noise from outside the castle.

"Oh no, what now?" said Granny George.

They went to a portal to see what was happening.

"Look," said Uncle Weirdo. "It's a boy on a motorized bicycle."

"It's Orville!" said Big Blue. "It's Orville!" She ran down the staircase, followed by the others.

Uncle Weirdo lowered the drawbridge and the boy from the telegraph office drove his marvelous machine into the castle. "Special delivery for Granny George," he announced… "for three telegrams."

Big Blue, after introducing Orville, invited him to join them, and to sample Uncle Weirdo's cooking. Orville happily accepted.

Granny George examined the envelopes and opened the one with the oldest date, looking very apprehensive. "I pray it's the good news we're all expecting," she muttered. But only a moment later she was trembling and sobbing, as she dropped it. "I can't read it," she sobbed, "it's just too horrible."

Big Blue picked it up. "Granny, look! This one is dated four days ago. That was before I sent my M-Mail. And Besides, Governor Billingsworth is only saying they're still missing."

"I'm... not sure I know what you mean," Granny George sobbed.

"Granny, you need to read the other telegrams." Big Blue picked out the second oldest one and handed it to her grandmother.

"You open it, Honey, I don't think I can."

"Telegrams will soon be a thing of the past," said Uncle Weirdo. "They're already being replaced by telephones. And my computeamajiggy will only hasten their demise."

"You may be right, Uncle Weirdo," said Big Blue, "but let's talk about that some other time." She read the message to herself, and then said, "Listen everybody, it's from Mother and Father, and I'll read it.

CENTRAL UNION TELEGRAM

Granny George
The Cozy Cottage
Dark Forest

Thank you BB. Directions great/found R.C. station/ all patched up. Wizard a phony. Leave Africa 3days by steamship. Home about 3 weeks/can't wait. Love to everyone/J&J

Now the old castle really rocked as they all celebrated. After much laughter and crying they all gathered for a group hug, capturing Orville right in the middle. Granny George, choking with happiness, hugged Big Blue and Little Red together. "Thanks to you two," she said, "that wicked witch is gone, and your parents are coming home. I'm so happy I could burst."

"Noo," cried Grandpa, "don't do that."

Big Blue couldn't hold back her tears as she kissed her Granny. "Thanks for trusting me, Granny. I love you."

Uncle Weirdo, smiling like a Cheshire cat, gave Big Blue a great bear hug. "You have made me happy beyond my wildest imagination," he said. "And coming from me that's saying a lot."

"Wait," said Big Blue, "there's still another telegram."

"Go ahead and read it, Big Blue," said Granny George.

Big Blue silently read it, and then began crying.

Little Red hugged her, "What's wrong, Blue?"

"It's just that I'm so happy," she answered. "It's from the Sheriff. Remember I called him about those wicked gnomes, and about Dwight?"

"Sure I remember, Blue, what does he say?"

"Well, in short, he says they captured all seven of them, and that Dwight and the other prisoners were rescued and will be okay. He says they're thinking about putting Dwight in a zoo for his safety."

"Do you mean the dragon?" asked Uncle Weirdo. "Was his name Dwight?"

"The very same dragon," said Big Blue. "I just hate to see him all alone and behind bars in a zoo, it's just too sad."

"Don't worry," said Uncle Weirdo, you won't have to. We'll bring him here where he'll be safe. He can roost on the roof. A dragon is just what my boring old castle needs."

That brought about another round of hugs, tears, cheers, and laughter.

"I have to be going now," said Orville, "but I'm happy for your good news. Can I talk to you privately for a moment, Big Blue?"

Big Blue sat with Orville in the corner of the parlor for a long chat. He then left the same way he came, with a RING, RING, RING, as he crossed the moat.

"What was that all about?" asked Little Red. "I'm dying to know."

Blushing, Big Blue whispered her secret to Little Red. "He wants me to go with him to the fair in Pigeonpoop, and he says this time he won't take no for an answer."

"That's awesome!" said Little Red. "I'm so happy for you."

"Thank you, Little Red. I'm happy, too, and this time I didn't say no." Big Blue and Little Red shared a long hug. "Promise not to tell anybody, Little Red, but Orville told me he and his brother are installing wings on his motorized bike and they think they can make it fly[52]."

"No way! I don't believe it."

"Well I do, they're really determined."

"All right," said Uncle Weirdo, "now it's time for you to entertain me. I'd love to hear about your journey through Storyland."

They took turns telling him. Granny George told about the witch, and she thanked Uncle Weirdo for providing the magic powder. "Oh!" she added, "we have something for you, Uncle Weirdo. It's a flying vacuum cleaner. We couldn't see how a toad could have any possible use for such a thing."

"*Awesome!*" he said, "I've always wanted one. And it's just as well too, that you took it-- just in case she should ever recover from the curse. And I see her magic wand is still strapped to it."

Everyone looked aghast, and were thankful that Grandpa Scaredypants hadn't heard Uncle Weirdo's thoughtless comment.

-->====((====<--

---

52 Fly—only eight years later, in 1903, Orville Wright and his brother Wilbur made the first powered flight of an airplane.

Story after story was told as they sat around the fireplace. Big Blue and Little Red were so close now you would think they were glued together. Wherever one went the other followed. Nothing could separate them.

Already, Chippy had explored every nook and cranny of the old castle. He constantly entertained them by popping out of a crack in the stone wall in the parlor, peeking out from beneath the kitchen stove, and always showing up when food was being served. Even Grandpa came to adore him.

Grandpa Scaredypants and Granny George sat at the kitchen table, engaged in subtabularinterdigitation[53], smiling, and whispering. Later, the enlarged family sat around the fire and talked into the wee hours of the night. Then they retired to their rooms in the turrets.

Much later, however, there was still a light on in one turret. A girl wearing a blue bonnet could be seen and lively music heard. The room was bouncing as she happily danced to the beat of the Rhinoceros Romp, klumpiti klumpiti klump. She twirled to the window and shouted down to the sleepy alligators, "I'm the happiest girl in all of Storyland."

---

53 Subtabularinterdigitation—holding hands beneath the table.

Determined is Luman Slade's first novel for young readers. His interest in writing peaked when he became a grandfather and began writing life-lesson stories for his grandson. Retirement then gave him the time needed to move to the juvenile fiction genre. He and his wife Jeanette live in Michigan during the summer months and in South Carolina in the winter. Visit him on the Web at lumanslade.com.

Anita Harmon, Illustrator
harmonthomas@ymail.com

After graduating in Art and Art Education at Northern
Michigan University, Anita Harmon taught in elementary and secondary schools in Michigan and Wisconsin.
She enjoys working in all areas of art. Many of her pho-
tographs were the basis for her paintings and watercol-
ors. She uses them to tell the story of people, places, and
times. Her favorite medium is acrylic, but she also paints
with oils and watercolor, draws with charcoal and ink,
does scratch art, and paints murals in businesses and
homes.

31167478R00112

Made in the USA
Charleston, SC
08 July 2014